For Pam

Acknowledgments

A sincere thank you to the friends and colleagues who read and re-read versions of this book. They include critique partner Gilly Segal, members of the Southeastern SCBWI, and the Columbus Scottish Festival and Highland Games, Columbus, Indiana. I am truly indebted for the patience and encouragement of my parents, my children and my loving husband. I'd also like to acknowledge the proud citizens of Fife County, Scotland, where an impressionable American spent two summers. The characters and events in this novel exist purely in the mind of the author. Any errors in historical and/or geographical content are entirely my own.

Slang in this narrative is taken arbitrarily and written in my own version of the Fife patois. I apologize for any errors in the brogue and welcome corrections via my blog at literarymom.wordpress.com.

One

Fife County, the backwater where Eileen Morgan would spend the summer of her sixteenth year, was across the ocean to nowhere. It occupied a forgotten corner of Scotland, had a handful of unremarkable whiskey brands, and served as free-range grazing for five hundred thousand lowland sheep. And on the county's south side sprawled the Forth Bay, and from its cliffs, when the fog lifted, you could sometimes see Edinburgh on the other side.

On this thistly portion of Britain perched a solemn building called the Red House, where Eileen's Granny Fran had just retired.

Edinburgh Airport was just as modern as Chicago's O'Hare, with fast-food restaurants, a nail salon, and tattooed teenagers slouched over smart phones. But the average age increased by fifty years the moment Eileen boarded the ScotRail train to Fife.

And things propelled downward, fast. The only food she'd seen in six hours rolled in via *trolley* with a bent old woman whose right hand cringed in spasms as she yelled, "Buffet!"

The buffet included two broken scones and something labeled "sausage roll."

Eileen leaned her head against the window and watched the tracks slide underneath the rail car. Things would get better. *Outlander* was filmed here. That roguish Sam Heughan might be casting about in need of a sausage roll or a side trip to Loch Ness. Eileen stretched for a better look at the water below the Forth bridge. No movie stars, though. No monsters. Just miles of iron gray water. Fog rolled in and steamed up

the window. Eileen had nothing to look at, then, but frayed blue uphol-
stery and a Newcastle Ale can rattling across the floor.

Besides her mother, Joyce, their companions were locals. The
man opposite looked frail, his hands wrapped around a walking stick
with a griffon head for a handle. The woman, his wife, Eileen guessed,
clutched a polka-dot umbrella and four nylon shopping bags, each full
of laundry. If these were the heroic folk Eileen's mom had mentioned,
the Bruces, the Macbeths, she'd rather have a teenage mugger.

Leven Station, the stop nearest Granny's village, was the third one
on the route. There'd be a mall, at least. Wi-Fi cafes. Maybe a vintage
record store. They were cool. She recalled the websites her mom had
pointed out, Edinburgh Ghost Tours, the World's First Golf Course.
There'd been rolling hills and wild ponies, outdoor pools, and fields of
clover. Maybe there'd be a cute caddy to flirt with. Even a Starbucks.

There was no Starbucks at the Leven Station, but there were a
handful of teenagers. Eileen brightened as she stepped down to platform level.

"Oi, watch it, knob end!" a girl in a school uniform shouted. She'd
been pelted with an orange backpack that another kid pitched out the
train door. The girl was about Eileen's age. She wore her plaid skirt
hiked to barely legal. Her top was untucked, and above it was an expensive-looking leather jacket. They shared a moment's eye contact. Eileen
looked away first. The girl in uniform was pregnant.

She blew a purple bubble in Eileen's direction, then picked up
the orange backpack from the platform and slung it across her back.
Another girl in matching plaid joined her from the Glasgow train. This
girl, blond and made up like a rock star, opened a pack of Pall Malls. The
two of them lit their cigarettes and sauntered toward the exit. They had
matching ponytails, one jet-black, the other white/blond, both pulled
so tight their eyes bulged.

"Goodness!" Joyce hustled Eileen down the platform. "Where is
that girl's mother?"

After clattering luggage through the station and into an underpass
that smelled of pee, they reached the lobby.

"You have change, right?" her mother asked. "To call my mother? You held my wallet in Edinburgh when I charged the rail tickets."

"Nu-uh! I was in that rank bathroom brushing off the skanks with the glue bottle," Eileen answered. There hadn't been any glue bottle. But she had run into what looked like a girl gang passing a cigarette back and forth. They'd been Gothed out in tight skirts and fishnets and had enough tattoos between them to start a biker club.

As her mom was about to scold, Eileen noticed a tidy-looking man near the exit holding a sign that read *Morgans*.

"That's us!" Eileen's mom waved. She dragged her suitcase across the lobby toward the man. "Morgans, right here. Are you a sight for tired eyes!"

Two model-waif girls looked up from a magazine they were sharing and sneered. When Eileen didn't pull her eyes away, one of them shot her a V sign with her fingers. "Up yours," she mouthed.

The driver put away his *Morgans* sign in a coat pocket and reached to take Joyce's suitcase. He left Eileen to drag her own bag to the parking lot.

"Great," Eileen thought. "Already invisible."

"Do ye prefer the radio or the news, ma'am?" he asked after they'd settled in the backseat.

"Do ye wish fir the windows to be lowered?"

"Is the temperature to yir liking?"

"Is the radio station all right?"

Joyce approved the music despite Eileen's glare.

One Direction, Mom? For real? Eileen opened her mouth to insist on a station change but saw Joyce's eyebrow: "grown-ups talking." Better to save it.

Eileen clenched her hands in her lap. She would study the surroundings, or the car interior. It was, let's be honest, an awesome ride. Reminded her of something Prince Charles swelled around in. The interior sat four people and had two benches you could pull down from a panel. The armrest between Eileen and her mother turned out to have a bar inside, one half with miniature bottles and the other with cubed ice. Far cry from the cup holders in the nine-year-old Jetta back in Evanston. It even had a tiny TV set attached to the ceiling behind the passenger seat.

As they pulled out of the station parking lot, the fog lifted, and Eileen could see about her for the first time. Leven was an old-time mining town. What appeared to have once been tidy, whitewashed cottages were coated with coal dust. Small grocery stores and mom-and-pop fruit stands stood on the curb while crumpled retirees struggled over the cobbles with grocery carts. Children idled in the street.

"What a hole," Eileen said.

Joyce glared. "Sorry," she made a face at the driver. "Sixteen goes unedited back home."

"If it's not to yir liking, miss," the driver replied, "you can lend a hand cleaning the place up, 'praps."

It *was* a hole. Anyone could see that. And no one cared when you said it about Gary, Indiana.

"Not much money for street cleaning since public funds dried up," the driver said.

Eileen turned to Joyce. "Is it all this...run-down?"

"Some parts. When I was growing up in England, these were successful mining towns. But in the seventies, terrible accidents happened—fires, explosions, strikes. A lot of families moved away. But some stayed and took new jobs. That's how the community—they call it an estate—where Granny moved survived. Lord and Lady Rutherford, who own the land and live in the castle, got their miners retrained as farmers and craftspeople."

"So there's a castle?" Eileen hadn't remembered that detail. Her mood went up a few notches as she considered the possibilities. Exploring the moat, discovering a lost cache of jewels, trying on gowns. "Is the castle where Granny lives?"

"No, no." Joyce laughed. "But it is next door to her. Been there since the thirteenth or fourteenth century. Don't expect it to look like Disney World, though. It was built as a fortress and is nearly empty. Just the old couple live there, and they don't get a lot of help. Your granny says it reminds her of a dungeon," she whispered. "Some rooms are said to be haunted."

They were driving through high hedge rows now. So high it wasn't possible to see the landscape anymore. But at the next turn, the foliage lowered, and a sign appeared: *Rutherford Castle Estate*.

Several miles of mixed-use farming came into view. Rich brown fields rolled into the distance, dark and newly plowed. On the other side of the road, ripening grain swayed. Sheep grazed and dozy lambs wandered the hillside. Their driver had to beep at several to get them off the road. As they made their way up an incline, a group of small, whitewashed cottages appeared. They were much cleaner than the ones in Leven.

"Thar's the house of the Stalkers. They take care of the land and the livestock. Caedmon's in that pasture." They passed a featureless field. "He's the laird and lady's prize stud."

Eileen had never heard of a *prize stud* before. It sounded like a sort of rural insult. She rose from her seat to look for the trophy-winning whatever it was. She couldn't see anything but grass in the pasture. Grass and a sloping tree. She was too shy to ask the driver who this Caedmon—or was it Caveman?—was.

"Just one family manages all this?" Eileen's mom asked.

The driver glanced in his rear-view. "That's right. Roun' 'ere, it's one family what does the farmwork."

Joyce gave Eileen an eyebrow. "And you say you have too many chores."

"Then there's the gardener, Mr. Temple, and the lord's secretary, Earnest Jenkins." The driver murmured something under his breath then. Sounded like *lickspittle*; A term Eileen hadn't heard before.

"How many Stalkers are there? Any kids?" Eileen liked Northern types. All the Minnesotans and Wisconsiners she'd met were cool. Laidback and never hurried, very un-Chicago. Two guys from Marquette had stayed with her friend Monica's brother last year on a soccer trip. And they had been cute and cuter.

"It's just three lads, miss. The late Mrs. Stalker died five years ago. And their da', poor bloke, died in a fall off the oil rig. Been just the three boys tending the farm ever since, with Hugh, the eldest, doing the looking after. They're often shorthanded. You'll go down and help, miss, when the there's extra work, I expect."

"But I'm sixteen!"

Joyce smiled and gave her leg a pat.

"Same age as our Ewan. He's been tending the stock since he was twelve."

"I'm here to help Granny unpack." Eileen crossed her arms smartly. "And then I'm due home for driver's ed."

"Well then, I'll mind my p's and q's."

Eileen looked over at her mom, who was trying to smother a smile. The driver didn't speak again for a while. Instead he turned the volume up on what was now Celine Dion. *Just two months*, Eileen promised herself.

How had she gotten herself talked into this? Monica would be out right now practicing for her driver's test. Her older sister Evelyn would be flirting with lacrosse players at her precollege class. And God only knew who Doug would pick up working at the ice-cream parlor on the Oak Street beach. But Eileen was good and truly stuck among the field hands and retirees. How had she allowed this to happen?

Two

Rutherford Castle rose on the horizon—a dawn of gray stone on the crest of a hill. It towered above a bluff overlooking fields in one direction and the Forth Bay in the other. Dark, tall, and impenetrable, it was more like a Roman wall than a private house. With the land cleared around it for farming, and no other buildings nearby, it hulked like a stone dinosaur.

Granny's house was the castle's nearest neighbor. Eileen recognized it from the real estate ad they'd gotten from Gran a few months ago. Even as they entered the driveway, a quarter mile past the castle, it towered in the background like a mountain. It wasn't pretty. It was straight and gray and orderly, with three floors of tall, uncurtained windows staring into wilderness.

Their driver pulled to a stop. Joyce and Eileen opened the doors.

Granny's new place was signposted —the Red House. Though built of similar stone to its neighbor, the Red House had been painted a deep wine color and was fashioned after a medieval tower. "A folly" Granny had called it in her letters. A fake medieval building made to look the same age as its thirteenth-century neighbor. Three floors of living space rose straight up from the ground with a crenellated edge at the roofline. The building, like the shorn, bare hills surrounding it, gave a mournful feeling, like it had once had lively occupants, ladies with summer dresses, kids at birthday parties. What remained here was a skeleton. A gust of wind peeled around the corner and something inside groaned, like a heavy chest being dragged across the floor.

The front door opened suddenly, and Granny Fran came out with her arms raised. Eileen hadn't seen her grandmother in two years. The last time was when she'd visited Evanston for Christmas. Her appearance took Eileen by surprise. Her hair, which had been abundant and waved with homemade pin curls, had thinned to a cobweb. She had narrowed, too. Her shoulders were rounder, her back more stooped. And as Granny approached, bundled in an oversized cable-knit sweater, Eileen felt a pang in her stomach. She *should* take an interest. Even though she didn't have Doug or Monica this summer, look what happened to the old folks when you hadn't seen them. Eileen's worry ebbed, though, as Granny produced a "Hello, girls!" and hurried to their car. Once set in motion, she was as sturdy as a cart horse.

"Joyce!" She hugged Eileen's mother. "How was the trip? Eileen, you've grown! What are you, thirteen? Was the journey awful?"

"Sixteen." Why was age so hard for adults?

"Not too bad of a trip. Mr. Clyde here has made things much easier." She reached into her wallet, got out a bill, and tipped him. He took the note, touched his hat, and placed their bags on the doorstep.

"If you'll be needin' anythin', ladies, you have the number of me mobile. I'm here aboots most days to drive Lady Rutherford." He nodded in the direction of the castle.

"It's high time we had tea." Granny turned to Eileen. "I hope you won't mind unpacking some cups. I've only unearthed the necessities so far. Can you look about for the boxes?"

The veins on Granny's arms showed glaringly as she leaned on Joyce's shoulder. They stood out, purple and knotted. How did you circulate blood like that? Especially in the cold? Would winters here be such a good idea? Granny had injured her back several years before, and when her housekeeper retired, she didn't want to manage a five-bedroom and garden by herself. However it had been steps from market and close to several friends. The Red House was miles from town and had three flights of stairs!

"Will this place really be easier for you, Granny?" Eileen was shown a group of boxes as they climbed a small stair to the kitchen.

She extracted a set of china, and Granny selected the cups she wanted. Then she sighed. "The retirement home makes more sense, eh? I have the benefit of the sea air here, and my cousin Rowena."

"Your housemate?" Eileen had hoped it might be a rumor, Gran having a strange old lady companion. "Is she here?"

"Reporting for duty!" Boomed a voice from below stairs, and soon after, a hill of a figure appeared on the landing. This woman was Granny's age, ish, but three times as wide. She wore a linen smock dress and macramé poncho. Her feet were in unmatched socks and Birkenstocks and between her sandals cantered a knotty brown dog, cowlicked like a guinea pig. As he leaped at the moving boxes, Rowena straightened her back and produced a toothy grin. Her teeth were the same gray as the Leven houses.

"Rowena at your service. Cohabitant of the Red House. Commander Emeritus, Southeast London's Women's Royal Army Corps, and gal pal of Granny Fran from the Ladies' College of Saxmunden."

She gave Fran a firm slap on the back, which pitched Granny forward a step, after which Rowena cleared her throat, picked up Joyce's suitcase, and marched it to a nearby bedroom. "Which of you belongs to this?"

"I do." Eileen's mom raised her hand.

There was a thud as Rowena deposited it inside a bedroom.

"You must be Joyce." Rowena returned to the living room. "Nice to meet you." She pumped Joyce's arm. "I'll help Fran settle, no worries. Made a good impression for her with the Rutherford side. They're my cousins," she added to Joyce. "And"—to Fran—"we'll keep each other from falling down the stairs, right, old girl?"

Both ladies burst out laughing.

"What about that tea, then? Eileen?"

She shuffled to the kitchen and filled the kettle. That Rowena. How did Granny unearth her? And for a roommate? Seemed a strange choice for someone as quiet and private as Fran. The kettle whistled, and Eileen poured the water in a teapot that already waited for her on the kitchen counter. She turned to find the tea bags but on her way to the pantry saw that the faucet was still on.

Strange. She was sure she'd turned it off.

She turned it off again, more firmly.

Then she let herself into the pantry in search of Earl Grey, what her mom usually drank. The kitchen wasn't the best equipped and was as narrow as their linen closet back home. There was green linoleum on the floor, in a sort of pond-scum color. And the countertops were eggshell-colored laminate, with putty over the gouged spots. The weirdest detail was the tin pipe faucet. No fixture on top of it, just plumber's piping. Same as what ran through the walls.

After the tea steeped five minutes, Eileen took the pot and four cups back to the living room. Granny was sitting primly in a red wing chair near the window absentmindedly massaging her left knee. She wore a purple shawl on her shoulders and contentedly looked at the view of the castle.

Well, she looks like she belongs here. Eileen brought the tray to the coffee table, and the women gathered in several nearby chairs. Eileen, her mother, Rowena, and Fran all poured for themselves. As she sipped, Eileen studied the motif on her cup. The china was chipped but still beautiful with its Japanese birds and bridges. She'd had a miniature one like it in a child's set. The story of lovers transfigured to birds.

"Now that you're here, Eileen"—Rowena stirred her tea—"you can help take care of Charlie." She nodded in the direction of her dog. "By the way, he's dying for a piddle." She then poured half her tea into her saucer and placed it on the floor. Charlie leaped at the plate, lapped up the remaining tea, and turned it upside down with his nose.

Eileen gave her mom a look, hoping for an excuse out of dog patrol. All she got in return, though, was a shrug. As Eileen got up to find the leash, she wondered if anyone ever argued with Rowena.

"Oh, and, Eileen," Rowena said as Charlie charged down the stairs knocking over a stack of dishes, "until we find the right moment to introduce you, stay clear of the castle."

"Why?"

"The laird's a little off his kettle. Had a stroke a while back. And he's never loved strangers, or the English, or children, or Americans. Your gran and I being Poms—err English—is bad enough. But an American kid on the property might bring him out with his stalking rifle."

"I'm not a kid." Eileen imagined a bearded geezer at one of the castle windows with his night vision. "I'm sixteen."

"Pardon me, madam. But six or sixteen, it makes no difference. If you're under twenty-five, the Rutherfords consider you a child. Except at the farmhouse, where they're practically family and the young ones grow up so fast."

Rowena took a slug of tea. "They'll see you soon enough, just that old man, he's known to have *episodes*. Used to look for snipers in the trees. Went right up and threatened that yew tree with his hunting piece."

After tea, Eileen went down to get the dog leash, as instructed. It and the extra rain boots she'd been asked to wear were inside "some old boxes" in the foyer. But so were the umbrellas, scarves, cardigans, wool hats, gloves, golf clubs, and raincoats. Charlie bounced around at her feet and in and out of boxes as she looked for gear, and he nosed his way out the front door before she could get the leash on him.

"Whoa, Charlie, where're you going?" She shut the door behind her, but the dog was already fifty yards away, and, yes, rolling in a cow pie. "Charlie!"

She wondered if she was going to end up washing him for Rowena later on. Then she wondered how much cow shit there was out here in the fields. She hadn't taken the time to change from her ballet flats. She'd seen the rubber boots but hadn't had time to change, and her pink Steve Maddens sagged like wet paper.

What kind of sixteen-year-old spent their summer minding grannies? Good thing Doug wasn't here. She'd never felt soggier, smellier, or less cute.

Three

I am the youngest person in the entire country, Eileen e-mailed Monica on her iPhone later on. It was nine o'clock. She'd fallen fast asleep at eight, with the jet lag. And then a while later, music woke her. Tinkly music. Nostalgic, like from a music box. Once awake there was no falling back to sleep, so she dug out her mobile again.

Monica
I found out yesterday that the old folks in the castle hate children. I guess they think that b/c I'm sixteen I'm going to take a dump on their golf course or whatever. Oh, and Granny's roommate is this overweight, boneyard know-it-all. I have to walk her dog every day in the rain—ducking, btw, in the bushes so the owners don't see me from their creepy castle. How are you and Tim getting along? Any spectacular fights? Have you seen Doug? Has he been at the Evanston beach? I'll bet that skank Valerie's stalking him. Oh, I almost forgot: Did you pass your driver's test? Write me! If this ever gets through.

Eileen

P.S. The best place for cell phone coverage is in my closet.

P.P.S. Their teeth really are gray!

XXX Eileen

Much later, in the hours before dawn, Eileen woke again to music. Along with the music-box tune there was a woman's voice. Her song was a lullaby, but Eileen couldn't tell where it was coming from. First it seemed to come out of the ceiling and then from inside the walls. And then from behind the window curtains. She hadn't heard this particular song since she was a toddler. Granny sang it when she couldn't go to sleep.

> Speed bonnie boat like a bird on the wing
> Onward, the sailors cry
> Carry the lad that's born to be king
> Over the sea to Skye.

She'd last heard that song in the pink bedroom where her mom grew up, its walls decorated in horse show ribbons, the middle aged face of her grandmother who stroked her hair and sang.

Eileen dreamed of Evanston that night. She was walking hand in hand with Doug, then driving with him in a midnight-blue convertible along Michigan Avenue, listening to Nora Jones, only she had a Scottish accent. At the stoplight, Doug put his arm around the back of Eileen's seat. He reached a hand around her shoulder and wound a lock of hair around his pinkie. "I like you in the driver's seat." His voice was growly and possessive. Then he smiled that prom-king smile, with surfer bangs falling over his eye. What would it feel like to run her fingers through that hair? He raised an eyebrow. He was going to say something. No, DO something. His eyelids lowered, he leaned in, his chin grazed her cheek. "Where'd you leave the dog leash?" he whispered.

Eileen awoke with a start. It was five a.m. Her internal clock was hours out of whack. From her bed, she watched through the window as the night faded from soft gray to coral pink. It was an early daybreak here in June, and yet the light rose slowly like smoke does from damp firewood.

Eileen heard Charlie bark. She got out of bed and started looking for sensible clothes. She hadn't brought anything truly warm enough. Her tank tops and capri pants made no sense here. Yesterday's temperature hadn't risen above fifty-eight. She would have to layer or else borrow that Inca poncho from Rowena.

What was that lullaby at night and all the running water. She'd have to ask Rowena if Charlie played in toilets?

The conversation from the car ride came back to her. *They say the castle's haunted.* She smiled. Maybe she'd been visited. But why would a Scottish spirit come to her? She wasn't glamorous or titled. She hid in shrubs.

She looked at the wall mirror above the bedroom dresser, ready to fix whatever might need adjusting—tangled bangs, frenzied eyebrows. A pale, ordinary girl looked back, sleep deprived but otherwise unremarkable. Her freckles made her look closer to thirteen than sixteen and so did the rosacea. *Firecracker,* her sister called her. *Emotional* was her father's word.

The hair was OK. Bangs not overgrown, bob still cute. Though she'd need to find some decent shampoo over here.

She bent over her suitcase. What did teenagers wear in Fife? Kilts? Houndstooth? She pushed aside her favorite organza skirt and a yellow halter-top and tugged on a pair of leggings and gray hoodie. Tying back her hair, she slapped on a Cubs cap and started down the hall.

Granny was already reclining on her wing chair by the living room window when Eileen came in. She put her hand on the old lady's shoulder. "Morning." They exchanged a kiss on the cheek. Fran was dressed in gray corduroy pants and green turtleneck. She held the newspaper open in her lap.

"Was someone walking around last night?"

"No. I don't think so. You might have heard my wireless. I listen to the BBC 'til a shocking hour. Sorry if it kept you up."

That might explain the lullaby. But the running water? "There was... well..."

"Hard time sleeping?" Granny folded her paper. The headline read "Rutherford Stud Wins at Sterling Games."

"Must have been jet lag." No sense bringing up ghosts with a frail old lady. And it probably was a talk show she'd heard in the night. Or the jingle from a commercial. The bright sunrise she'd seen from her bedroom had tarnished to gray, now. She sighed at the view from the living room. "Does the sun ever stay out?"

"For part of the day. But you can't count on it. Brits just pack their wellies and get on with it."

"Wellies?"

"Rain boots," Rowena clarified.

Eileen turned her head sharply at her sudden voice. Rowena was on the stairs with a tray of toast. She set it down on the coffee table and switched on Granny's radio. A reporter chirped his headlines, Highland tattoo (whatever that was) postponed a fortnight, sheep trials on at St. Andrews, weather, twenty-three degrees with periods of rain.

Sounded arctic. But of course, the temperature was in Celsius. Eileen would have to figure out the conversion one day.

"Why don't you make tea, Eileen?" Rowena suggested through a mouthful of toast. Crumbs sprayed the floor. Charlie hurled himself on them. Pointing downstairs with her elbow, Rowena added, "I stuck the matches on the shelf to the left of the cooker."

Yes, ma'am. Eileen slowly rose. *Allow me, ma'am.* She dragged herself down the stairs. *Can I take the tray if you're done with it? And walk your dog when I've done doing dishes?*

She found yesterday's teapot on the drainer along with four cups and saucers. She then picked up the kettle and lit the "cooker." As the water came to a boil, she looked for milk—since the grown-ups required it with tea. There was no carton in the refrigerator. Not on the counter. She looked in a few cabinets.

"Gran, there's no milk!" she yelled up the stairs.

"Outside the front door."

Why didn't I think of that? Sure enough, when she opened the door, three glass bottles stood on the doorstep. They were the old-fashioned single pint size. They looked like glass bowling pins. Each had a foil top, two silver and one green. Something had torn a small hole in the green one. Charlie? A bird? Eileen hoped whatever it was wasn't swimming around still.

"That's the half-fat one." Granny arrived at Eileen's shoulder and pointed at the green-topped bottle. "I never touch it, but the birds like it."

They climbed back up the stairs and took the tray Eileen had prepared to the living room. "We're lucky the milkman comes all this way. In winter, the roads are snowed in. We'll go to the castle for milk then. The Rutherfords get Jenkins, their butler, to bring the shopping in some sort of a tank."

"It's an ATV, Fran," Rowena corrected.

Know-it-all, Eileen thought.

A few minutes into breakfast, Eileen realized she hadn't seen the TV set yet. "Where's the TV?"

There was a pause. Joyce sighed deeply.

"Oh. Television. I had one in France." Rowena looked like she was remembering a summer fifty years ago. Before climate change. Before cell phones, when teenagers asked their elders questions. "It had very poor reception. There's an old set in the shed, I think. Saw it last week. But it looks older than me."

A hard place was gathering in Eileen's stomach. "Is there someone who can hook it up?" Eileen looked at her mother, who was slowly shaking her head. But her shows! *True Blood. Dancing with the Stars. CSI.*

"Eileen. This is the countryside." Joyce rose from her chair and approached the three-stair stepladder Fran had placed by an inset bookshelf. "Even if we got an old TV installed, there isn't a satellite tower for miles. Your shows would all be white noise."

"But without a tower, how do you get online?" She turned to Rowena. "Or make a phone call?"

"Phone works fine." Rowena pointed at a blue rotary on the end table near the window.

"That's a landline. What about your cell phone? And your computer?"

"We have a typewriter under the china cabinet." Granny pointed at a corner closet. "But the ribbon's dry."

Calm. Eileen closed her eyes. *Don't freak. You had AT&T bars last night.* To keep from saying something really nasty about yokels and the Dark Ages, she speed-walked to her room and ducked into the closet. She sat down hard against the wall and covered herself in clothing, the gypsy skirt and diaphanous blouse she bought specially for this trip."

Who the hell was all this for? What was she doing here? She tugged out her iPhone. Three bars on the display. But there was no message from Monica. No text from Doug. Had she disappeared completely from real life? She was in a closet in the butt end of nowhere. Might as well be in the grave.

Stuffing her phone back into her pocket, she returned to the living room. "I'm going to walk the dog."

She stuffed her feet into the nearest pair of boots, which turned out to be a man's, and marched Charlie out the door. Spraying gravel with every step, she made her way through a tumble of long grass, through the circular yard that edged the driveway and went straight up the nearest hill. There, while Charlie yanked on his leash, she pulled her cell phone out again and dialed Monica's number.

She'd be up. She never got up later than ten on a summer morning, all those north-side beaches to hit and street fairs to wander with cute earrings and summer dresses. It was, what, three o'clock back home. Her call went straight to voice mail though. The heck? That never happened at home. Something must be messing with her service.

Charlie suddenly yanked hard suddenly. Eileen lost her balance and slid into the soft earth of a molehill. Her oversized boots collapsed the mound and her entire left leg disappeared to the knee inside the earth. She dropped Charlie's leash and watched helplessly as he charged into a field of waist-high grain.

"Charlie!" But he was gone.

Hauling at her leg, she managed to extract her foot and hopped around the field, kicked wads of mud into the air. Then she crouched in the grass to find her phone, which she'd flung somewhere during her fall. It was next to a tuft of overturned grass, Monica's face shining from the ID display and a tan line sneaking from her spaghetti strap. Eileen grabbed the phone and sat back hard in the wet grass.

So that was it. She was off-radar. Stuck with dog patrol and Rowena the Tooth for the rest of the summer. And all the while Monica swanned around in hot summer outfits, driving her parents' MG. The closest Eileen would find would be shotgun seat the farmhand's tractor.

"Pardon me, miss."

Eileen shrieked, dropped her phone in the grass again, and jumped up. In front of her, amid the waist high grain was a boy in a raincoat carrying an armload of fleece. With the hood of Granny's anorak pulled halfway over her face, Eileen couldn't see very well. She tugged her hood down. But as she did so, she slipped again in the grass and went down.

"Easy." The boy set down the wool he was carrying to steady her. "Give a care in the wet." He grasped Eileen gently by the elbow. Only then did Eileen realize that the fleece he'd been carrying was a live sheep. A lamb, in fact. It sat on the ground, legs curled like a sleepy cat, blinking its huge black eyes.

"Adorable!" Eileen lowered her hand to pat the lamb. But then she stopped. Might not be the custom, petting someone's sheep. Looking at the boy, though, Eileen felt a pulse of adrenaline. He was cute, in a disheveled way. He had overgrown rusty hair and a constellation of freckles across his nose. He must be one of the farm boys. "Thanks. Um, my name's Eileen."

"I'm Ewan."

"Like the actor?"

"Like the actor." He rolled his eyes.

"Sorry. I'll bet you get that all the time. He's just the only Ewan I ever heard of." She was talking too fast. "Um, do you live around here?"

"On the farm. We watch the Rutherfords' animals, me brothers and me. What do you do?"

"Well, right now, I'm looking after Charlie. But he runs away every time I put him on the leash."

"He's got shepherd in him, that one." Ewan smiled at Charlie, who had reappeared in a nearby thicket of trees, where he snarled at a squirrel. "Maybe you'd lend him sometime. Our dog retired."

"Sure. Only..." She paused.

"Only...?"

"He belongs to Rowena, who's new at the Red House. She and my granny moved in there. I'm in town to help them get settled."

"That so?"

"And for brewing tea, walking dogs, and bringing in the milk."

"Do the Rutherfords know you're aboot?"

"Um, what?"

"The laird and lady. Have they met you?"

Eileen didn't know how to reply to this. The laird didn't like kids. She was supposed to avoid him. This boy seemed to be employed here, and he might not like outsiders, either.

"Yeah," she said haltingly. "I met the Rutherfords yesterday. But I don't think we'll be hanging out too much."

Ewan laughed. "Not hanging oot much? That's grand. You're right aboot that, Miss. The Rutherfords haven't *hung oot* for nigh on forty years. No one really knows them. He's just about bedridden. You sometimes see *herself* through her car window. She takes the air in the Bentley. But the closest she'll come to shaking a stranger's hand is to lower her tinted window a half inch. If ye really met her and his lordship already I'd be surprised."

Eileen's neck felt shrunk. Stupid, stupid to lie. She wanted a friend. Tell the truth, damn it. Here was a chance.

"So what do you do around here for fun?" She was desperate to change the subject.

"Fer fun? Oh, fer fun there's a wee pub, the Wharf, down the docks in Leven. They do fish-and-chips and have a juke box. But we ne go to the pub very often. There's a lot of work here on the farm in summertime. By evening we're fair ferfochen."

"You go to the fair?"

"No, no." He laughed. "*Fair ferfochen* is Scotch. It means we're tuckered oot. Tired? From tendin' the beasties?"

"Oh. Who's we?"

"Och, that's me and me two big brothers. Danny's the planter, family cook and odd-jobs man. I tend the sheep. And our Hugh's in charge of dairy and the bull. He's a legend, our bull, Caedmon. Shall we walk a bit, miss? That dog of yours'll be on t'other side of the hill by now."

"That Charlie." She shook her head.

They began walking along the ridge together.

"I've never had a full-time job. I've had a couple summer jobs—babysitting, working the counter at Dairy Queen—but I've never been on a farm before." Wow. She was flirting with him!

"You get used to it." Ewan let the lamb run along next to them. It was slower than Charlie, but it trotted to keep up. So cute!

"Me brothers and me," Ewan went on, "we been on the fields since I can remember. But we go to school in the autumn. I went to boarding school in Edinburgh for three years. Until they needed me back." Ewan paused a moment, put two fingers to his lips and made a piercing whistle. Charlie dashed from a thicket, tail wagging. Ewan lowered his lamb onto the ground and made a tiny gesture with his hand. Charlie clearly understood. He nudged the lamb into a trot, then led it in a small circle from Ewan's side to a nearby tree and back again.

"You'll have to show me how you did that!" Eileen said.

Charlie sat down with a thump next to Ewan, who rubbed his head in affectionately.

"There you go, Prince Charlie." He took a gnarled, leathery rawhide out of his coat pocket and offered it to him.

This puzzled Eileen. "You know him already?"

Charlie sank into the rawhide like Thanksgiving after a two-day fast.

"He's been on the estate for years. Makes the rounds, picks himself a new keeper every so often. No one knows how old he is or who he belongs ta. Yer gran's friend, Ms. Rowena, has had him awhile, but he'll hanker after someone else eventually."

A gust blew by and rustled the barley stalks.

"I'd better take him home." Eileen shivered. She hooked the leash onto Charlie's collar and pulled her hood over her head. It suddenly occurred to her how unkempt she must look. Without a shower this morning and no makeup on, plus the mannish boots and old lady raincoat she must look practically homeless. If she'd known there was a chance of cute boys, she would have put forth a little effort. Touched her cheeks with blush at minimum.

Charlie pulled on the leash.

"American, right?" Ewan said suddenly.

"What?"

"Yer accent. It's American?"

"That's right."

"I could tell. I watch *24.*"

"You get that?"

"Course."

"You get cable out here?"

"We have a satellite dish. And Wi-Fi. Hugh has a sat phone fir foul weather, too. You never know when a squall kin roll off the Forth. Why are you looking at me like tha'?"

Eileen's heart began to pound. This guy was cute, funny, and he had two hundred channels. "You don't know how happy you just made me."

"That me brother has a sat phone?"

"That you have some...technology. I'm boarded up with two old women who pronounce it *Internut.* And I haven't gotten a single e-mail since I got here."

"Must make you homesick."

It began to drizzle, and the already weak light was fading. Better go in before it stormed. Ewan gathered his lamb back into his arms.

"Meet me tomorrow and you can come home and watch our telly. Or you can try me on yer phone. Here's my number." He showed her the display panel on his own phone.

She punched it quickly into her Contacts. "Thanks. I'll try it. Only place this seems to work, though, is in my closet."

"At our place"—he started down his side of the hill—"it's on the loo."

Four

I met a boy, Monica, Eileen e-mailed her friend late that night. *His name is Ewan Stalker. He has red hair and freckles, kind of like Prince Harry. Only more serious but not in a nerdy way. He's totally rugged. You should have heard him whistle for Charlie. He picked me up when I half disappeared down a molehill. So polite. But not all "Pass the crumpets," more "mind the puddle." If he's been working the fields all these years they probably consider him a regular grown-up at the castle. Hey and listen—he said I could watch his family's TV! Since there's no chance Gran's getting wired up anytime soon, I'm gonna take him up on it.*

How's the good life? Been to any concerts? Got a great tan yet?

You know, I've decided something. If Doug is seeing someone, don't tell me about it. Unless it's Valerie. No, don't tell me even then.

XXX Eileen

P.S. Did you know that Ewan is Scottish for "well-born"? I looked that up in something called a heraldry text.

P.P.S. I had to ask Ewan to explain what he was saying like fifty times. Scots have their own language, practically. And they really don't like the English. They call them "Poms." Americans aren't as bad as Poms, but everyone still calls me "Yank."

Five

Eileen woke to the sound of tapping. At first from directly under the bed.

"Pipe down, Charlie," Eileen murmured.

The tapping turned to scratching.

Eileen groaned and leaned over to extract Charlie from under the bed. But he wasn't there. She turned the light on. No Charlie anywhere. Feeling a little creeped out, she nestled back in the blankets. Rats in the paneling? Squirrels? Roaches? Even gatehouses got infested.

She woke one more time before dawn, this time to distant music. Not a humming voice but a bagpipe. It was a sweet, mournful sound like you heard at an important funeral. It was so peaceful, though, that Eileen fell to sleep again almost immediately.

Six

A week later, Eileen had been to Ewan's hillside every day, but after seven walks up the muddy slope with Charlie, she hadn't seen him once. She'd been too shy to leave a message on his voice mail the couple times she called his mobile. He was the guy. He was supposed to make the first call.

She cleared her throat after lunch. "Granny. Do you know Ewan?"

"The Stalker boy?"

"I guess so."

"Yes. He's a sweet chap. You've met him, I take it? Well, I heard from Daphne—that's the castle cook—that everyone with two hands is helping with the calving. It's that time of year. And it's a big job. If you go down to their barn, you'll probably find the lad. Don't be surprised, though, if he's busy."

Eileen wasn't sure if she wanted to see a cow give birth. She'd practically stopped breathing when they'd dissected fetal pigs in the spring. But she hadn't met anyone her age except for Ewan. And though Monica would never stoop to do so, it was probably worth it to make the first move. "Is it OK to go down to the farm?"

"Why wouldn't it be?" Rowena answered from her card table. She was busy with a crossword but always had time to add to nearby conversations. Always.

"Well"—Gayle sucked her teeth—"you said I'm supposed to stay under wraps. Being a kid and all."

"The old man isn't on the farm today." She dusted the last crumbs of a teacake from her mouth. "And he wouldn't set foot at a calving.

He's much too grand. Anyway, now that you've met Ewan, you're more or less introduced. Once someone new is on the estate, it's as good as a BBC bulletin." Rowena raked a hand through her hair. "You won't run into the lord. *He* doesn't leave the castle. The peasants might see him in his wheelchair, and that wouldn't do." She winked. "You could run into the lady, but she's a softie underneath. Have fun!"

"Why doesn't the lord like young people?" It seemed impossible even for a lord to avoid under-twenty-five-year-olds.

"He and the lady like them well enough in...moderation. They had three daughters of their own. The two older girls moved abroad. They lost the third, tragically, and ever since they've been anxious about accidents. The summer of Emily's death was chaos. It was the first summer I spent at the Red House, more than ten years ago now. The tears and curses that day. The will torn up. It was a mess. Lord and Lady Rutherford didn't leave the castle for three years."

"How did she die?"

Rowena motioned for Eileen to step closer, where Fran, who'd begun to doze in her wing chair by the window, wouldn't hear. "The bull charged her."

Eileen clapped a hand over her mouth. "Caedmon?"

Rowena nodded. "Mowed her down on the lawn right there."

"Right in the yard?"

Rowena nodded. "Got loose from his field. Broke out, they say. Was overstimulated during breeding season. In fact, folks say—" She was interrupted by a crash overhead.

"Oh, for God's sake." It was Joyce. "Charlie! I'm going to put you in a pie!"

"Charlie's down here," Eileen yelled at her through the floorboards. The dog looked on from his spot on the couch, his pink tongue lolling.

Silence followed. A few minutes later, Joyce joined them from the storage space upstairs.

"There's something...peculiar in the attic." Her gaze roamed to the ceiling. "I was nowhere near that set of glasses, but they leaped off the shelf, right in front of me, and shattered."

Joyce was really shaken, something Eileen never saw. Hair askew, fingers trembling.

"And was that you giggling?" Joyce turned to Eileen. "Not bothering to come out of the corner when I asked you?"

"I haven't been in the attic."

"Well"—Joyce pursed her lips—"you gonna help me tidy up or what?"

"You don't have to yell."

As she helped with the glass shards, she almost said something about the sink disturbance and the lullabies. But then grown-ups assumed something was wrong when you started on that train of thought. Then they your phone away or your allowance. She'd shelve the bagpiping poltergeist for now.

Rowena had established KP rotations, and lunch had turned to Eileen today. She turned for inspiration to the kitchen shelf where she found *Cottage Cook*. On page 28 was a succulent looking "meat pie," which sounded awful, but better than "blood pudding" on page 56. Or "bubble and spit" right next to it. Shepherd's pie was on the inside back cover. Eileen had eaten it once or twice. And Ewan was a shepherd. So shepherd's pie it was.

She peeled potatoes, slowly, sitting in her mind's eye with Ewan on a sunny hillside, a picnic basket between them, watching Charlie chase an errant flock of sheep. "More shepherd's pie?" she'd ask.

"If you kiss me, first," he'd say, and seize her, hoist her to the hay wagon and...

"What's for lunch?" It was Joyce.

"Shepherd's pie." Eileen rummaged through the refrigerator. "There're onions and carrots and this." She held out a wrapped package. "What's 'mince'?"

"Ground beef." Joyce took the bundle. "I can help with the spuds." She wrapped a '50s-style apron around her waist. It was faded but carefully ironed so the frills stood out, the kind of thing Granny might have worn during war time, when she was a Women's Auxiliary Air Force officer.

With Joyce peeling the potatoes and Eileen heating onions, meat, and carrots, they made quick work of it, finishing with three whole pies and extra potatoes on the side.

When they finished their meal, Eileen made the bold suggestion: "Maybe I'll take one to the Stalkers." Very unlike her. Not a Monica move at all.

Rowena went for it, though. "Take Charlie with you, and—"

"Stay out of sight. I know."

"I was going to say try not to let him off the leash. Now that you've met a Stalker, news will have reached the castle. The old man won't shoot you for delivering a pie."

Eileen wasn't so sure. As comfortable as Ewan was on the estate, everyone else here watched his back. So until she got an invitation from the castle, she'd stick to the high grass.

Seven

High grass turned out to be increasingly mosquito-clogged as the Scottish summer progressed. And it gave terrific cover to cow pies. This gave way to wandering thoughts on the theme of Caedmon. What kind of fence did his paddock have? He'd killed the youngest Rutherford daughter. Might he be at large this very minute with a pack of wolves on his heels and a dementor bringing up the rear?

She came to a clump of trees on a crest between the Red House and the Stalker farm. She rested there and eyed the horizon. She could see beyond the bluff, down the cliff and over the Forth Bay. The fields stared back dull and treeless. Not a sheep or field hand anywhere. Was she the last person on Earth? The last queen of Scotland?

Charlie barked from a few yards downhill. Eileen made a face. "You just got to be leader, huh?" The clouds lifted off the slate-dark bay for a moment, and for an instant, the Forth Bridge poked through. The highest suspension bridge in Europe, Rowena boasted. The same stretch Eileen had crossed on the train from Edinburgh. City slickers on that side, poor relations over here.

On the downslope of the hill the Stalker's farm spread out, four buildings, each a whitewashed two-story with colorful flower boxes. A barn stood a little apart with a neatly raked corral, and a tidy gravel road lead past the whitewashed buildings out to the main road. As Eileen studied the buildings, a familiar animal galloped into view heading in the direction of the barn. She looked down at her hand where her leash lay slack.

"Charlie!"

The compound was silent when Eileen reached it. No sign of her runaway sheepdog. She hoped he wouldn't interfere with the calving. It took her a little while to find Ewan's door.

"Hello?" She neared the stable where a side door leaned partially open. She poked her head in just in time to see the edge of someone's hat and muddy boots. "Um, hello?"

The man didn't reappear. Best to try another door.

She tried the farmhouse next. Over the doorway was a placard reading *Stalker*. She rang the doorbell. No answer. "Anyone home? It's Eileen. I brought shepherd's pie."

Still no answer.

She moved to the building next door. It was identical to the Stalker house, but slightly smaller. She knocked on four doors by the end of it, getting no reply at any of them. Strange. Lights were on in each house, and the stereo was on in the largest.

Eileen turned to retrace her path across the fields when she heard something. An animal, distressed, wailing, like someone had beaten it. It was coming from the barn. That must be where they kept the animals.

"Mauuuuuh!" the wail again. Bloodcurdling. Then there was a bang. It rattled Eileen's teeth. She could leave the pie on the doorstep. But Charlie was still down here somewhere. Rowena didn't like him to be out at night. And it was already evening.

"Charlie!" She turned a slow circle. "Charleeeee!" Why was no one around? She'd pictured a calving like an Amish barn raising, crowded, rowdy, barbecues and lemonade.

A bark sounded inside the barn. Its door rested a few inches ajar. Eileen approached and peered in. Sure enough, Charlie was pacing back and forth between two men—the other Stalker brothers, she guessed, both of them crouching over a prostrate cow. The animal was slick with sweat and panting.

"Watch the hooves!" A figure in coveralls jumped back. He was a tall fellow with scars on his face, gaunt but with muscular shoulders. Then a second guy with Ewan's coloring came into view. He maneuvered quickly at the head of the cow, but didn't notice Eileen outside.

A third figure stood up from from the shadows, close to the cow's hindquarters. His freckles were unmistakable.

"I've helped as much as I can." Ewan tugged off his latex gloves. They were streaked red.

"Good on ya." The other men both clapped his shoulder. The scarred one unzipped his coveralls partway, stretched his back, and started toward the door. Eileen ducked behind a nearby trough to hide. Though she'd like to see Ewan, she didn't want the brothers seeing her. Not yet. There was something about the tall one that bothered her.

But Eileen's trough was just too short.

"You there!'" The man stepped toward her but stopped at the barn door and leaned against it. He slowly unpacked a cigarette and perched it on his lip. A scar discolored his brow. It was about a half inch long and stretched from his temple to his ear. Sort of like a rope burn. He wasn't going to talk to her, she realized, but wait for her to show herself. Not the friendliest way to meet a person. But whatever. She slowly stood to her full height. Then, not knowing what else to do, she sat on the edge of the trough.

Ewan's brother didn't look her in the face, not even after she sat down a couple feet from him. He struck a match on the barn door, lit his cigarette, and forced a jet of smoke out his nose.

"You're the Yank?"

She nodded. Not sure if "Yank" was insulting or not.

"Well, if it's Evan yer after, he's a fright." He lowered his Marlboro and pivoted 90 degrees. "Oi! Ewan. Foreign girl to see ya. But wash up. She's keen to run."

Blushing furiously, Eileen clutched the shepherd's pie. What had she been thinking bringing pies? He'd have a jibe for that, no question. She wished she could get Charlie to bury it.

"I was just looking for Charlie—my dog." Her voice sounding shrill and stupid and young.

"He's in with Ewan. Ain't he a one? Always there for the birthin' and dying'. Sorta creepy if ya think aboot it." He dipped his hands in the trough, then to wash the blood off.

"Did you happen to see Temple just now?" he asked.

Eileen plied her memory for someone who could have been *Temple*. "I saw a man in a duck into one of the stalls."

"That's the one. He's the castle gardener but he's always hanging aboot the farm. Can't decide his profession, that fella."

"Hello, Eileen."

She startled. It was Ewan. Half his chest exposed under unzipped coveralls. "Uh, hi, Ewan!" She fidgeted with her shopping bag. "Sorry to barge in but...I think Charlie's...I came to...I brought..."

"It's all right." He reached a hand to her shoulder, then saw the gore on his forearm and withdrew it.

"I made...um...shepherd's pie." She unpacked the pie dish. It had been packed in a Tupperware container, and after the long walk, it had recombined into a dark orange porridge. She held it out. What else was there to do? She wished she could drown it in the water trough.

Ewan took the container, then stared at it a good sixty seconds without speaking.

"Oh, wait." Eileen put her hand to her mouth. "It's ground beef. What's the matter with me! After you've been working so hard to deliver..." she trailed off.

"No worries." The larger man tapped ash onto the gravel. "He eats anything. The dolt just isn't used to female attention. But you'll get over it, right, little brother?"

There was a groan from the barn. Ewan smiled at Eileen, placed her Tupperware gently on the ground, and ran back inside. Then over his shoulder: "You can join us."

As she started in their direction, a grating sound stopped her. The Rutherfords' Bentley had approached almost silently behind her. Inside it rode the lady. Eileen was certain of it, though she could see nothing of the occupant behind the tinted windows. The rear window lowered half way and a woman's hand appeared. It was covered with a black satin opera glove and it rested on the lowered pane. Waiting. Unmoving.

Eileen sucked her breath. Hide in the bushes? Inside the trough? As she was considering wedging herself under the barn, a cheer came from inside, and Eileen spun on her heel.

"That's the spirit!" Ewan shouted. "A wee bullock!"

Eileen saw the black glove tap its index finger a single time on the top of the window and then withdraw. The tinted glass slid back into place, and the Bentley made a cumbersome U-turn in the courtyard and drove back the way it came.

Eileen ran almost the entire way home, towing a complaining Charlie behind like an anchor. Well, no more ducking behind bushes. The old lady had seen her. The jig was up. She reached the hilltop where she and Ewan first met and paused, clasping her knees to catch her breath.

Charlie, who wasn't in the least winded, looked gleeful through his matted hair. *Cheer up*, he seemed to say. *They like you.*

"Not that you'd understand," Eileen said, "but I just blew my first impression."

"You Yanks and your impressions." Out of nowhere, a stranger appeared. But just his back. His face was turned to the woods directly south. All Eileen could see of this new arrival was his tight-fitting suit jacket. The grass reached his waist and hid his lower half. He wasn't a tall man. About Eileen's own height, in fact. He'd materialized like an elf from the forest.

"Who are you? I should tell you." She pulled Charlie close. "I have a guard dog."

He turned to face her. He was lean and pink-faced, about forty-five, in an expensive coat and swinging a walking stick. The heather-gray tweed of his outfit blended perfectly with the hillside. Eileen wondered if he'd been following her. Dressed like that, he could have been watching for an hour or more without her noticing.

"That's no guard dog." The strange man straightened his tartan necktie. It had an "R" emblazoned on the knot. "It's the mongrel that snatches game birds. And you ought to know who I am, now that you're staying, as I suppose you must. I'm Earnest Jenkins, caretaker of the estate. And *you*"—he leaned toward her—"you're a Morgan."

Someone had informed him, then.

"A Morgan." He cracked a tendon in his neck. "From a backwater."

"From Illinois!"

"From nowhere! Morgans, in case you didn't know, are boarder-landers. They're known in these parts for seven generations of freeloading."

Though stung, Eileen didn't contradict. The tone of this guy was, well, it was menacing. Like he'd been slighted somehow by her family. As far as she knew, though, she'd never met a Jenkins. She pulled Charlie closer. "I don't know what you're trying to say, mister." She took a few steps closer to the Red House. "I'm on my way home. And I'm not bothering anyone."

"You have no business here." He licked his teeth and seemed to calm a little. "And much as you come and go,"—he smoothed his cowlicks. There were several, front, back and side —"with that animal and ostentatious yellow raincoat, you are on the land of Laird Rutherford. Without the castle's invitation. So be careful." At that last statement, he poked Eileen's shoulder on each syllable.

"Ow!"

Charlie snarled.

Jenkins retreated a foot and dusted something invisible from his gray-green sleeve. For a tidy man, his nails were surprisingly full of dirt. He looked across the horizon then with narrowed eyes. "And be careful when you're out and about. Never know what's on the prowl."

He smiled a thin smile and smoothed the boot-black hair once more. He turned, took a few steps, then added over his shoulder, "There's been a few to interfere with us before. Maybe you've heard what happened to them."

Eight

"I've been made."

"What?" her mother frowned as Eileen slumped on the couch.

"Lady Rutherford saw me. And just now I ran into some guy in a uniform tie who said I wasn't sanctioned by the castle, so I guess you'd better pack me back to Chicago." She slumped down on the couch and started nibbling from the package of digestive biscuits that was open on the coffee table. Everyone knew her now. The Stalkers, the Rutherfords, the driver, the castle butler or whatever. What was next, MI5? But, really, it was for the best. She wasn't welcome here. The goon on the hillside made that clear. And it wasn't like she had a bunch of friends in town. If she went back to Chicago now there would still be time for driver's ed.

"OK," Joyce chimed in, an armload of laundry in front of her. "A run-in with the lady doesn't mean it's quits. But that butler does sound strange. You haven't picked her roses, have you?"

"No!"

"Calm down. We'll just go on as usual. You didn't take Charlie anywhere off-limits, like the old coal mine, right?"

"I took a pie to the Stalkers, remember? That's when Lady Rutherford turned up."

Rowena walked into the living room at that moment midway through a phone call. "I will, Lady Rutherford. Yes. I understand." She replaced the receiver on its cradle and sat down next to Joyce.

Eileen stared at her. No one spoke for a moment. A thrush rustled in the trees outside, and the clock in the hallway gonged.

"Is that the time?" Rowena asked. "I'm starved. Who's for fish-and-chips?"

"Rowena." Joyce set the shirt she was folding firmly in her lap. "Is Eileen in trouble for turning up at the farm?"

"On the contrary. She called to compliment *the young lady*." Rowena nodded in Eileen's direction. "She wanted to know the name of the American girl who'd come to watch the calving. There's not many teenagers who'll dirty their hands with outdoor work these days, especially with a calving. Did you see it born? Lady Rutherford said you looked quite involved."

Eileen laughed. "I didn't see anything. I was too busy trying not to get in the way. I was about to take off home, in fact, when the Bentley showed up with Lady Rutherford inside. I never even saw her face. Just a black glove."

"That'll be her." Rowena nodded.

"So she isn't mad?"

"The Rutherfords are all mad as hatters, dear. Have been since the closing of the coal mine. But if you're asking if she's angry, then no. The laird might throw his stick on the floor if he saw a stranger near his newborn calf, but *she's* still got her wits. She's rather pleased, it turns out, that we brought a teenager who doesn't spend all day banging at the video games."

"Oh." Wow. No more skulking around. She could go see Ewan in plain sight. There was still that weirdo with the slicked-down hairdo to consider, but he was scrawnier than her bulimic cat back home. She could handle him.

The next morning, for the first time that summer the sun was out. It positively blazed. By ten, it was tank-top weather. Eileen had to strip off her anorak and go inside to change. Charlie bounded in every direction, delighted at the change in weather. He found two finches arguing over a caterpillar and chased them in circles until they flew into the branches of a tree. The tree was home to a squirrel, who screamed a torrent of abuse and sprang down the driveway toward the castle.

"Not THAT way," Eileen yelled as Charlie made chase. Even though she'd been given the OK from Lady R., that Jenkins guy had been so rude, she was nervous about Charlie running into him, digging, maybe, where he wasn't supposed to.

She jogged after him, right past the castle's first-floor windows and toward the garden. *Don't look inside.* But as she crossed in front of the last windowpane, her eyes strayed. There wasn't much to see through the glass. It was coated in dust. No one had cleaned the panes in months. Made you wonder about that Jenkins. Whole place could be a total tip. Or empty. It was a single couple there. Could be they lived with nothing but two recliners and a radio.

Eileen slowed to a walk, now that she'd cleared the windows. She was enjoying looking at the ramparts, now. Up close, with no one telling her to duck for cover. The walls were red-gray masonry with moss gathered between the bricks. Creepers grew where mortar ought to be, and in several places, it nearly covered entire windows. Everything was straight and ridged, though. Three rectangular floors rose up from one another, nothing added or embellished. No sculptures, no balustrades, no variegated roofline, just blocks of stone fused to one another, like an enormous rocky flyswatter.

Actually, if it hadn't had a crest of swans above the main doorway, Rutherford Castle would have looked like a prison. Eileen guessed it was done on purpose. Feudal lords would have needed their castle battle-ready. Still, if they ever did get a visitor here besides herself, they should consider curtains, maybe even a pool.

Eileen had totally lost Charlie, but she could hear him barking somewhere ahead. Remembering how Ewan called him, she put two fingers to her mouth and blew. A shower of saliva flew out but no sound. Must take a trained shepherd to pull that off.

"Charlie!" Ah, she saw him. On top of a ledge alongside the castle garden. "Get off that wall."

He'd followed the squirrel up an embankment and onto a crumbling stone wall. "Come down now, Charlie. We're no allowed up there."

"Actually, you are allowed." A few yards away there lounged a stout man in his sixties. He was wearing a green jacket, a kilt, and a fisherman's cap, similar to the one Eileen had seen on the man who'd ducked out of sight in the Stalkers' stable. Today, he had his pruning shears at his side and half a row of bushes neatly trimmed. Nearby stood a wheelbarrow of tools and sacks of mulch. He had a trim goatee and a small pipe that rested unlit in the corner of his mouth. He gave Eileen a smile and extended his hand. "It's easier to get through this way."

"I'm allowed over the wall?" She asked. "Isn't it private?"

"Not this bit of it. I should know. I'm the estate gardener—Brian Temple. It's a public park from the barrier wall 'ere down to the beach. That bluff and the estate are owned privately by the Rutherfords. But the walled garden, the forest, the caves, and the beach below are open to visitors. It's taken care of by the National Trust. Been that way now some eighteen years."

"I'm Eileen Morgan. We almost met yesterday."

Mr. Temple narrowed his eyes a little.

"Down at the Stalkers' stable? Right before the calf arrived?"

"Mmmm, don't think so, miss. I was at a flower show all of yesterday." He looked away, then titled back in his boots and surveyed his wheelbarrow.

Eileen cleared her voice. "Well...I was chasing my cousin's dog just now. He probably went over the wall."

"He'll be down by the water. Dogs love the beach. Take my hand. I'll pitch ye over the wee stile."

A small space had been left in the rock wall where Mr. Temple was pointing. In it were two wooden crossbeams, one on top of the other.

"The stile keeps free-range animals on this side, and allows humans to cross to the other. Half a sammie?" He offered Eileen a small wax paper-wrapped package.

Go on. Let down barriers, she coached herself. So she reached for the sandwich and took a bite. It contained scrambled egg and a layer of something sweet, like barbecue.

"Thank you." She bit a nanometer of sandwich and tried not to wince.

"Your dog Bonnie Prince Charlie's a real explorer," Temple said, chewing his half sandwich. "Likes the caves, too. If you don't mind a wee stroll, you'll find him either there or along the path to the beach."

"How did the caves form?"

They've been there since before any Rutherfords. The castle's built right on top. Pirates used to hide inside them and there's been ancient carvings found in one. There's a rumor we have Norse rune stones on the property. Ever hear of them?"

Eileen shook her head.

"Runes are the some of the oldest artifacts in Britain. The oldest were made by Picts and can be huge, like Stonehenge-size or tiny, to carry around on your body like an amulet. The Picts were mysterious, thoo. They left no records other than the stones. They are the original Britons, here even before the Norse. Their carvings show how communities lived, what they ate, how they worshipped and fought and died. What was valuable. Their race birthed the clans of this country: the MacIntyres, Douglasses, and Rutherfords. So their runes are the fingerprints of ancient Scotland."

The old man sighed and scraped flecks of mud off a trowel.

"What happened to them?" They'd never studied Picts in high school. Normans, a little. King Henry VIII, but not the Picts.

"The Romans. Routed their religion and ruined their land. What remains today is cleared, treeless land for farming. The only artifacts left in the end were the carvings that couldn't be burned. And wouldn't you know"—he rubbed his forehead—"the few good ones remaining are in the British Museum. In London."

They were quiet awhile. Mr. Temple lowered his head. Eileen wondered if he was praying. Or crying.

"Right!" He snapped to attention, a smile on his face suddenly. "Been takin' up far too much 'a your sightseein' time. You best go find yer hound." He motioned for her to climb over the stile. "Have a gander at the cave, too, right?"

"Nice meeting you." Eileen took his hand and hopped the stile. "I liked hearing about the Picts. My granny and Rowena would, too. They're real history buffs."

"Och, Rowena. She knows everyone. I help out at the Red House when things need mending. Gotta do by yer relations, you know."

"You're related to her?" Eileen asked.

"By some cousin. We're all some kind of Rutherford around here. Some just more titled than others. Give me best to the ladies."

"I will," Eileen replied. "Thank you, Mr. Temple." She paused a moment, though. "Has anyone complained of noises at night, in the Red House?"

"Is it skittering feet? Like the wee rats?"

"Well..." Eileen twisted the button of her anorak. "Not so much squeaking. There's...music.... it's been keeping me awake at night. And random faucets turning on. Creaking floorboards. Probably a passerby with a loud car radio, right?"

"There are no passersby at night," Mr. Temple said slowly.

Eileen knit her fingers. "Or maybe just my gran in the hallway."

He didn't reply. His face had turned from a medium mushroom color to bleach white. But then he smiled. "If the noise is at night, chances are ya got yirself a rattie." As he spoke, though, he was opening and closing his fist around the trowel.

"So...a mouse or a...squirrel?"

"Unless it's the castle spirit. Some folks see her—the Rutherford Ghost—while they're here. I think you've heard about our Emily?"

Eileen nodded. *He* knew about her, too. Seemed everyone did.

"She's known to visit folks at night, especially if they're new." Mr. Temple began packing his gear. "Or if they've made her angry. She likes visitors, unlike many here," he added with an eye to the castle. "It's a curious ghost. Sort of aimless. She never throws pots and pans as far as I know."

Were there Scottish ghosts that *did* throw pots and pans? Eileen hoped she hadn't annoyed Emily. Rowena's army-issue cookware looked like it could put your lights out.

"Enjoy the walk." Temple wheeled his barrow toward the garage where the Bentley parked. "Say hello to Charlie."

Eileen cleared the stile and started toward the caves. Something had really creeped Mr. Temple out back there. Maybe *he'd* been haunted. He clearly believed in the Rutherford ghost. Maybe she *had* thrown pots at him. After all that talk about Romans and clearing Scottish land, he seemed a little paranoid. Grown-ups. Why were they so weird? That probably *had* been Mr. Temple hiding behind hay bales at the Stalkers' farm. Why was he pretending it wasn't?

For her part, Eileen liked the idea of ghosts. She'd been on the Haunted History Tour of New Orleans. Marie Laveau, Hoodoo, undead sightings at the cemetery. Great stuff. A dash of that variety might turn a Scottish summer into something memorable.

The forest this side of the stile was truly beautiful. It spread a quilt of blue bells, snowdrops, and lilies of the valley. Giant beech trees arched their limbs overhead, and in the distance, whitecaps churned the bay. The lower she got on the path, the brinier the air became. It was a rough water, the Forth Bay, capable of violent storms. Fran had vintage postcards of it on the walls of the Red House, battleships struggling against the current, breakers snatching at the deck in ten-foot sprays. Eileen could well imagine pirates coming to land during high sea and hauling up treasure to bury under a forbidding cliff.

A large root caught Eileen's boot suddenly, and she flew face-first into the dirt and leaves. Grit filled her mouth. *Please don't be a broken tooth.* She got up and felt the inside of her mouth. A cut had formed where her teeth clamped down, but nothing seemed loose. She spat a wad of dark saliva at the woods.

"Such a lady," came a familiar voice.

Ah. Finally Ewan. Eileen did her best to suppress a smile. He had Charlie by the leash, of course, and was leading him toward her down the path.

Eileen dusted off her shoulders. "I'm actually an heiress back home."

"Yeah, you struck me as an A-lister. Especially with the footwear."

"Oh, these? They're a man's, turns out. And the coat belonged to some groundskeeper. I'm doing a study of colorful native people for a summer project. But I have to eat at all the dive restaurants, too. Got any White Castles?"

He laughed. "We have Wimpy's. You know, bender-in-a-bun?"

That sounded awful. But those bender burgers didn't interfere with his teeth. They were perfect. Square, straight, polished.

"Or, if you're a vegetarian, they do a fine plate of chips."

Would he be a firm kisser or sort of shy? Eileen wiped the remaining grit from her mouth with the back of her hand.

"You just smeared yourself in blood, Dracula. Here." He handed her a handkerchief from his pocket. It was monogrammed with two cursive letters, *ER*.

She wiped her face. "So?"

"Better."

She handed back the handkerchief.

"Yours, now."

"Thanks." She put it in her pocket. "How's your new calf? I'd liked to have stuck around the other day, but Lady Rutherford showed up."

"Och, that's where you went. The lady's onto you, eh?"

She nodded. "It was gonna happen, right? Oh, and I just met the gardener, Mr. Temple? He's got an axe to grind."

"Don't get me started." Ewan rolled his eyes. "Everything that's wrong in his world is because of the Romans or the Poms."

"He said the Red House is haunted."

"Did he, now?" Ewan raised an eyebrow. "How'd that come up?"

Woops, the ghost was Ewan's deceased mother! Or supposed to be. Probably not the best thing you bring up with the guy you have a crush on. "Well"—she scratched her chin—"there's these creaking floorboards in the house at night..." She trailed off, hating herself to the core.

"Which room do you have?"

"The small one on the third floor with the red curtains."

He pondered a moment twisting Charlie's leash. "That room's got history. Have you seen the caves yet?"

Eileen was dying to know more about the ghost, but information was unlikely to come from him. "I was on my way there. Are we close?"

"Just around that corner." He pointed to an outcropping of rock ahead. "On the underside of the castle." A few yards from where they stood was a wall of masonry. Alongside it, the path descended sharply. "It's rank in there, but if you don't mind, they're well worth a look."

The path became increasingly hard to navigate. What had once been a well-worn footpath was now narrow and weed-choked. Waves crashed over her shoulder. The sea must be on the other side of the ledge, but the forest was so thick here she couldn't tell where she was exactly, nor how much rock held the forest up, and where it fell into the bay. Her boots skidded on a wet leaf. She caught herself, barely, on a tree limb.

"Anyone skewer themself back here?" She tried to urge a smile into her voice, but the terrain was more than uncomfortable.

"Folks don't bother with this route so much." Ewan nodded. He didn't seem to notice the incline, though, and he never once steadied himself against a tree. "It was once a shortcut to the mine. But the explosion closed everything down. For a while, Mr. Temple was finding needles on the path and in the cave. He closed all the mine entrances then. But the pirate cave had to stay open because it's National Trust. Then when the oil rigs started hiring offshore, the idlers cleared out."

"So we're not going to run into a bunch of thugs?"

He smiled. "Don't worry, just because they made *Trainspotting* here doesn't mean we all shoot heroin. In Glasgow, different story. But we're in the country here. There's a bit of boozin', but no more than you have in the States, I 'spect."

"The only drug use I know is girls in my homeroom with their mom's Xanax. I don't see why anyone would start the hard stuff, though."

"Probably because they don't have any choices in their lives," Ewan said, rather sharply.

What was his problem? "Isn't there always a choice? I mean, between doing something and doing nothing to improve yourself? Even the unemployed folks in my hometown—and there are a lot—shovel driveways or rake leaves for spending money. A drug user is never going to amount to anything, and they're a drain on society. Plus drugs make you look so bad—your face, your teeth, your hair."

"You've met my brother, I see." Ewan pushed his bangs roughly off his forehead.

Oh crap. *That's* where he was heading: Hugh was a drunk. She should have realized—that scar! He did look awful.

"Um." Redirect, Eileen, redirect..."Leven's a small town for an educated guy. Ever think of striking out? You know, travel a little?"

"Like you?"

45

"Well, I'm visiting a retired relative. I don't know that I'd call it travel."

"I'm here for family, too." He stopped walking to retie his hiking boot. "Even if I left the estate, my family needs me. So whatever university or career plan I set up would go and get shifted. Not much sense making for the horizon when you're born a farmer. Sooner or later, duty calls. Birth a calf, heal a sheep." He picked up a wayward shell from the forest floor and threw it hard into the trees. "Or bury the dead."

They were quiet for a few paces.

"Here's the cave." He put his hand out in warning. "Watch yourself!"

Nine

The cave entrance was absurdly low. They had to crawl to get through. The ceiling remained low for several yards before Ewan took her hand and let her know it was safe to stand.

Eileen straightened slowly and strained her eyes trying to find some detail in what had become near total darkness. "Where are we?"

"Directly under the castle and right above the bay."

Ewan struck a match. For a moment, the interior frothed with light. The cave walls glistened, wet trails sliding down in rivulets. It was a narrow cavern, about twelve yards long and seven feet tall, and piles of earth were mounded against the edges.

"That's where the excavators dug last year," Ewan said. "But they didn't find much." The match went out. "Ouch! Burnt me finger."

"Let me see." Eileen grasped at his injured hand.

"You can't see, remember?"

She found his fingers and touched them gently. "Which one is it?" The darkness seemed to bring something out in her. Daring? Madness?

"This one." He put his index finger in her palm.

"The whistling finger." She felt his other hand slide over the nape of her neck. A muscle trembled somewhere in her abdomen. Her pulse roared.

Her body was shaking now. Did she go on talking or wait for him to kiss her? "Did anyone live down here?"

"Pirates. Hermits. Pre-Roman people. The researchers who mounded all that earth found a fourth-century carved stone in Aberdeen and took it back to London. When they came here, they brought loads of equipment, underground sonar, metal detectors, the lot. But no one found ancient artifacts here. Are you interested in this?"

"Are you?"

He ran his hand gently down her shoulders and rested it on the small of her back. Eileen wished she could see his face.

"Do you have another match?" she breathed.

Slowly, he took his hand from her back, and the room came to life. He removed an envelope from his pocket and lit the corner. A blaze lit up his face again. "See any carvings?"

"No. But that might be something." She pointed to the ceiling where a series of yellow marks shone against red sandstone. Looking closer, she made out what looked like numbers. "It's graffiti. Pretty recent, too—*Emily Rose, 1968-1998*. Nothing historic."

She looked back at Ewan. His head was lowered, and his expression had changed.

Emily. She kept showing up. "Are you all right?" She placed her hand lightly on his shoulder.

The last embers of his envelope burned out.

Several hours later, after dinner and a lukewarm bath, Eileen set up her closet IT hub. To her astonishment, there was an IM waiting from Monica. Nothing really heartfelt, but...

Yo, E. What up? Your farmer crush work out? -Mo

I think I blew it.

OMG, trying to reach you for days. Bet you didn't blow it.

The only service is in my closet.

So what happened with the hot shepherd?

I keep sticking my foot in my mouth.

Dude has baggage. BTW, Doug has been flirting with me.

Uh, what brought that on, Mo???

He lost his barista job. When guys are mad they do stuff w/o thinking.

Like what?

I told him I'm spoken for, but there was elbow contact, knee touch. You know.

The hell! Some friend! And yet for Monica kissing accidents happened a lot. Even with her friends' crushes. Eileen should be mad. Slamming doors mad. But she wasn't. She would have been six weeks ago. But Eileen couldn't picture Doug well anymore or hear the sound of his voice. Now that she'd held Ewan's hand in the dark and hid in shrubs to avoid old men, Doug-and-Monica seemed a little trivial.

But Monica! Eileen screwed her eyes shut. Then opened them as the bing of a new IM came in.

You know, Eileen, you should blow Doug off when you're back. Guys are so into that.

It was pointless to reply. What was done back home was done. Punishing her friend over cell phone would get Eileen nowhere. She powered down the phone and dropped it into her suitcase. They deserve each other, Doug and Monica. One made awful coffee, the other flirted with her BF's crush.

That night Eileen heard the bagpipes. But when she sat up in bed, it was gone. She smiled as she turned the pillow over. Bagpipes played for victories, right? She wasn't sure yet what she'd won, exactly, but something had switched on since yesterday. A deal-with-it-ness she hadn't had before.

49

Ten

Sometime before daybreak, Eileen awoke to creaking floorboards. She poked her feet out of bed and barely withheld a shriek as they touched the icy floor. She stuffed her toes into socks and clambered over to the door for a sweater hanging on a hook. Funny. She'd closed the door last night yet here it was ajar. She closed it, pulled a sweater over her pajamas, and climbed back into bed.

Minutes afterward, water sounded overhead. Not just dripping but a geyser. Like both sink faucets were on full tilt along with the shower and bath spout.

"Mom?" Eileen called. Directly overhead was her mother's bedroom.

The toilet flushed, but there was otherwise no reply.

"Gran?" Eileen whispered.

Silence.

That ghost has a thing with water. Most people would be alarmed by possessed bathrooms but she was getting used to it, even a little excited. An actual visit from Emily might be next. That would put her really close to Ewan. His mother had played guitar in life so listening to her in the plumbing might have some importance.

The next day at the Red House was all about gardening. Granny decided to plant summer vegetables so they'd have English peas during the lockdown winter months. Not knowing much about Fife County earth, they asked Mr. Temple to advise, and he came over early to get them started.

He got busy with herbicides and topsoil. As he worked, Eileen noticed that his hands trembled. And when he came and went for tools from the wheelbarrow, he stumbled several times. Could be a drinker or early stage dementia. Maybe he'd heard Emily's ghost, too. Got a cast iron pots thrown at him. If so, it was decent of him to help out around here—chief haunt of hers and all.

Eileen got orders from Rowena to trowel a vegetable row, so with some mismatched gloves, she began her trench. Joyce joined with the watering can, and Fran sketched garden designs and sorted seeds. Meanwhile, Rowena set herself on a golf chair. Though it was barely overcast, she wore an enormous rain slicker, like Eileen imagined you'd wear on a BP oil tanker in the gale of the century.

"Straighten that row!" she barked as Eileen struggled with the hoe. Already there were blisters under her work gloves.

"It is a straight line. See, I planted there, there, and there. Straight."

"Pretty disoriented formation." Rowena yawned. "Good thing your troops aren't going to war." She took a bite out of an apple. "Keep at it. You'll get it eventually."

"Yes, Mussolini."

"I'm not deaf," Rowena said.

They planted tomatoes, peas, crooked neck squash, potatoes, string beans, and radishes. Eileen covered the beds with fertilizer and Mr. Temple made a final pass with earth-friendly fiber mesh.

Eileen stood up and cracked her knuckles. Her back hurt in thirty places, but the sun was out. Her skin was sticky, and her face gritty and damp. If she'd been home, she'd have gone to Oak Street beach for a swim.

"Care to see the Rutherfords' garden?" Temple asked her. "It's shady there."

Eileen turned to him. Interesting. He was smiling now and tapping ash from the bowl of his pipe. He unrolled his tobacco pouch and put a plug in. All his earlier discomfort had disappeared. "Finished here for the day, I think. Might be nice to see how the swells do in."

"The Rutherfords have a garden? And are you sure *he* won't mind if I'm there?"

"I doubt it. I bring my niece now and then. That stuff about 'no kids' is pretty unofficial. It's Jenkins's rule. To *keep the undesirables at bay.* To *protect* the laird. In his younger days, Lord Rutherford had a temper, too. But that's long ago. Since the accident, he sleeps fourteen hours a day. Jenkins makes like he hates the world entire, but that ain't true. He's tired, and he likes to be left at his fireside."

Mr. Temple seemed to like the lord, Eileen realized. And she went with him to the garden despite Joyce's pursed lips. The warm air was doing something to her now. The fear was lifting, and so was the resentment at leaving home. Today, Eileen might even say she liked Scotland.

"Right this way." Mr. Temple pointed out a path along the close cropped castle lawn. They passed the low windows Eileen had hurried by on her way after Charlie. "You reach the garden from the bay walk, under the wee wall you were sitting on t'other day."

"After you." Mr. Temple unlatched a gate hidden behind some creepers. It was fixed into the stone wall. Inside the gate was an unremarkable courtyard with white pebbles on the ground and a dry fountain at its center. On three sides were gray, four-story fortresslike walls with few adornments.

"One more door," Temple chirped. Eileen saw a much fancier passageway on the other side of the courtyard. A tall, wrought-iron gate waited for them festooned with flower and swans. Engraved on the arch was the phrase *A Qui Appartenez-Vous?* And under it a truly spectacular view.

"Oh, Mr. Temple!" Eileen had never expected such a hidden jewel. And it was more than that, really. It was a fairy tale. Paths made of diamond-shaped paving stones led in various directions under an arbor of climbing roses. Gold, fuchsia, and scarlet blossoms assaulted Eileen's nose. Down the first pathway, a round lawn opened with a life-sized chessboard mowed into the turf. And on it topiaries had been carved in the shape of game pieces, a single pawn making its first move.

The circular lawn led to a display of fruit trees awash in blossoms: apple, cherry, and pear. And in a stone loggia hung an explosion of honeysuckle, where ecstatic bees were swirling.

"Why are they hiding this?"

"Och. It's not really hidden. The gate yonder's never locked. But, aye, it can appear a bit off limits."

"No kidding. Are the Rutherfords afraid of vandals?"

"Not really, miss. You see, the castle has always had a garden. Since medieval times. It was a mess until the current Lady R. replanted it. She's a real green thumb. There she is, now."

Yes indeed, there she was, getting up from her gardening cushion. Dusting off her hands. Straightening her cardigan. Approaching them this very minute, trowel in hand. Ready to smack Eileen a good one across the...

"Hello, Mr. Temple." She had a surprisingly gravelly voice. She brushed a strand of hair from her face with a bare hand. No opera gloves. "I see you've brought the American. Good afternoon, Eileen. Nice to meet you properly."

Eileen went limp with nerves. How did you greet a Lady? She bent at the waist, threw both arms wide, and tipped forward. The hood of her anorak flopped over her face and the dog treats she carried in the front pocket spilled onto the ground.

"Very nice to meet you, Mrs...."

"Lady," Mr. Temple corrected.

"Lady Rutherford. I hope you don't mind...Mr. Temple thought it would be OK..."

"Don't worry, dear. I'm joining the new world. Did you hear?"

She hadn't heard, but the knot in Eileen's stomach unclenched a little.

"Rowena and I have spoken," Lady R. continued. "I hope you'll enjoy yourself on the estate."

Eileen managed a nod.

"Excellent. Mr. Temple, if you'd be so kind, I'd like to take Miss. Morgan for a stroll. I don't expect she's been to a castle garden before."

Eileen shook her head.

The gardener put his palms together and gave a tiny bow.

"Lady Rutherford," Eileen said at last, "it's very nice of you to show me around. I know the lord doesn't like young people."

"It's been sorted out." Lady Rutherford looked squarely at her. "You're a bit of an exception here, not being family or staff. But I know you'll not disappoint me." She reached out and gave Eileen's hand a squeeze. "The estate's interdiction of children was a precaution, Eileen. We've had accidents with young people. And, well..." She waved her hand vaguely in the direction of the fields. "I don't want to have to send Jenkins to pull you out from under a plow. There he is now. Hello, Jenkins."

The butler stood in a nearby doorway. He had no walking stick today but a scarlet riding coat, jodhpurs, and knee boots. The ensemble made him look a good fifteen years younger. Was he a foxhunter? Eileen heard it was outlawed. He carried a leather messenger bag over one shoulder and a pair of riding spurs.

"You there!" He frowned at Eileen. "What's your business?"

"My invitation," Lady Rutherford answered.

Was she grinding her teeth?

Jenkins turned a glare at Mr. Temple next. But without comment, the gardener grabbed a rake and began scraping at the pebble court-yard. Jenkins seemed to have no more to say. He strode to the side door of the castle and disappeared inside.

Eileen turned to Lady Rutherford. "Uh, is he always—"

"Don't get me started," the lady interrupted, flapping her hand in Jenkins's direction as you would an insect. She chased her renegade hair back into place. "After my husband's stroke, Jenkins came up with a list of precautions." She directed Eileen to follow her into an orchard. "No children and all that. But it's a bore of a tale. Let's hear about you. Ewan's given me some background, and our Mr. Temple has been fol-lowing your family. Seems you take an interest in the farm!"

"Yes, ma'am. I do."

"You like Ewan?"

Eileen felt herself blush purple.

"And you're here to help your grandmother. Not just to take snap-shots and play Nintendo?"

"Yes, ma'am." What she wouldn't give for a DS, though.

"The effort you've shown to help your grandmother is admirable. Few teenagers are willing to do that nowadays. They're off to college, to travel or build microchips. They don't come back to Fife, Eileen."

"Your children don't visit?"

"No, dear. They don't. The young generation left Scotland. All we Rutherfords have now are distant relatives hanging on coattails." Here she narrowed her eyes at the place of Jenkins's departure. "Our future was going to be the mine. But look at that relic." She gestured at the forty-foot chimney that stood overlooking the bay. "Most productive coal mine this side of Aberdeen fifteen years ago. Now home to eight varieties of migratory bird."

Lady Rutherford had stopped walking so Eileen did the same. They were standing at the foot of a chapel built right into the garden wall. Next to it was a tiny cemetery. Eileen followed Lady R. inside the boundary, but given Rutherfords' propensity to wander in the afterlife, she didn't like disturbing stuff in there.

Only six or eight headstones stood at this site, all eroded, some defaced with graffiti.

"Angry miner families." Lady Rutherford pointed at the scrapes across one stone.

"Your employees' families?"

"I wish we could have given better compensation."

Eileen couldn't read much of the inscriptions. Some of the stones were shoved to the side, and there was a musty smell in the air, like the cave underneath them. Maybe that's what it smelled like to be cursed. Like corruption, spoiled tissue, and the like. Wow, this was getting morbid.

"I should go." Eileen twiddled a strand of hair. "I'm supposed to be pulling weeds at the Red House."

But the lady wasn't listening anymore. "Here's a dear one." She rubbed the top of a newer headstone with her forefinger. It stood squarely in its resting place, unlike the others, its inscription not yet weathered away. *Emily Rose Rutherford, loving daughter, & mother, 1968–1998.*

"How did she die?"

"She was reckless. But look, new flowers." A fresh bouquet lay at the base of the memorial. Field buttercups. No decorator's tape or baby's breath.

"That dear boy." Lady R. shaded her eyes and looked toward the bay and added "He fixed a tear in the lord's hammock the other day. Always making gestures. He's a noble spirit. If things had been different..." She trailed off and started up the path toward the castle.

Eileen knew better than to follow in her wake.

She walked home in a daze. After the windup of the century, Lady Rutherford was sweet. That and dying for company. Plus—shocker—she doted on Ewan. Strange, though, that the relationship between them was so formal out in public. Was that just how nobles treated the working classes? And wasn't Ewan actually a baron or something? His mom was born to the castle. That must give her son a pedigree.

As she made her way back over the hill toward the Red House, Eileen passed what appeared to be an out-of-use potting shed. A grove of small trees stood to one side and slightly behind. The copse of trees were low and gnarled with bristly leaves, but in the clearing between them, Eileen saw the obsequious Earnest Jenkins. She tiptoed behind a sprawling yew to avoid him. He was such a bore that she didn't want him spoiling her afternoon at the castle. She didn't have much to worry about, though. He was hunched over with a spade digging furiously in the earth. He looked up just once at the castle before he patted down the earth and placed something green on top. A piece of moss or tarp. Probably burying the lord's best tartan.

She tucked her neck as far inside her collar as she could and scuttled home by way of the hedgerows. How had that guy taken hold of this place while being *such* a snob. Good thing Eileen had the lady on her side. But even having scored that coup, she'd keep her distance from the secretary. Lady Rutherford even seemed afraid of him.

Granny was leaning over a box of winter clothes when Eileen returned, labeling umbrellas with masking tape. "Appears brolly's sha'n't be borrowed." And then in a whisper, "I took Rowena's umbrella yesterday. Got a dressing-down this morning. I'm labeling this one 'poor cousin' so there's no more mistakes."

Eileen felt a wave of fondness for her gran. She reached out and hugged her.

"Oh, my lamb. Such a nice cuddle!"

"Can I help you with those?" Eileen took a pair of broken boots from under Fran's arm. Why had she waited this long to visit? Granny was eighty-five, and when she went, there were not more grandparents in the family. She should do something to remember the trip by. Find the Morgan tartan or try to paint Fran's picture.

Lady Rutherford seemed to bring something out in Eileen, an urge to appreciate things. She would do that. With Ewan, she had a great example. But Eileen drew the line at appreciating Rowena. She fully expected the old bird to pay her eventually for the weeks of dog walking.

Eleven

"Why are we going to a pub for dinner?"

"So you can see the locals." Rowena pulled her coat on and urged the others down the stairs. "I thought you teenagers loved chips."

Granny and Joyce begged out. Fran had an upset stomach, and Joyce was tending her.

A pub, as far as Eileen could tell, was a bunch of retired guys loitering with their fifth beer. Not a great place for women, Americans or the English. "There's still leftover meat loaf from last night." Eileen tried. But Rowena wasn't dissuaded.

"I forgot to walk Charlie. He really looks like he needs to go."

"We're going, Eileen, and that's that." She shoved Eileen toward her car. "In you get." She slammed the front seat doors behind them and jerked her Volvo into gear.

"Off we go!" yelled Rowena, teeth bared. She floored the gas pedal and roared out of the drive in a spray of gravel.

Monica wouldn't set foot in a Leven fish-and-chips. No less than a Gold Coast cineplex would do for her. That's where she'd met her boyfriend, Tim, at a late show of *The Extraction*. They'd started necking right there in their movie seats. Never mind that six feet of intestine on the screen.

Eileen was pretty sure there weren't any movie theaters in Leven. But there were caves. She thought back to the match, Ewan's singed forefinger. His hands had been so warm against her neck. What would his lips feel like? Would he smell like cut grass? Salt water?

Rowena was midway through a lecture on a Norse myth. Some goddess named Loki had come ashore, yada yada yada. Eileen snuck a look at her SMS in-box. Nothing new from Monica. But would it kill Ewan to write her? He could get her number by just asking her mom or Fran.

"Of course the clans people forgot about Loki after the arrival of Christianity..."

"Uh, Rowena?"

"What?"

"We're near the Stalker farm. Maybe Ewan would like to come with us." Eileen strained to see the farmhouse through the dark. Though there wasn't much to see, she noticed two figures in the pasture, one tall and ambling, the other in a fisherman's cap.

"Does Mr. Temple work with the animals, too?" Eileen gestured at the shadows through the window.

"Not often. He's a full-time gardener 'sfar as I know. Could be branching out. Or maybe Hugh needs a hand today—look, there's old Caedmon." Rowena slowed so Eileen could see the infamous bull.

Eileen's skin prickled. She hadn't seen the bull yet. But just a fence away was the real thing, calm as you please and sauntering toward the men. He seemed sleepy, almost dragging his hooves. His head was lowered, not like he was going to charge, though. Just like he didn't have the energy to pick it up. It hardly seemed possible he could gore people. "Does he always look so bummed out, Rowena?"

"I don't know." Rowena rubbed her chin. "I see him in the pasture now and then. And he is typically more alert. Maybe he's unwell."

Hugh had taken Caedmon by the collar. He and Temple were in animated conversation. Something wasn't right. Hugh flapped an arm dramatically in Temple's face and added, "Not now!"

Temple grabbed Hugh by the sleeve then and pulled his ear close. A second later, the two of them turned toward the Volvo. Eileen lowered herself below view.

"It's all right." Rowena put the car back in drive. "They're done arguing. What those boys get up to at night with a cow. Don't even like to think."

Eileen pushed herself back into sitting position. Enough to see Hugh returning the bull to his stable, the animal still dragging its head. Mr. Temple had in hand now a small black steer. He brought it alongside Caedmon, who sniffed the new animal from shoulder to knee and then snorted, satisfied.

"Ah." Rowena pulled the Volvo back onto the Leven road. "Socialization. They're out to improve Caedmon's manners."

In Eileen's side-view mirror, Hugh lingered in the stable doorway staring after the car. She couldn't see his face at all, but she knew he was watching. Evaluating. Was he dangerous? Had Caedmon kicked him in the head? There was that scar above his eye. But maybe it was from a bar fight. She'd seen movies where London rockers got into brawls with broken bottles. And in spy movies, villains always give the eye that Hugh had just leveled. Bet he has a criminal record. Could she ask Ewan? Of course she couldn't. But maybe she could find out another way.

"Man's a runaway brick wall," Rowena muttered, pulling up to the Wharf Public House.

"Who?"

"Hugh Stalker, of course. And he likes his wee dram of ale."

She backed the Volvo into a parking spot. As they eased to a stop, Eileen noticed Mr. Temple climbing down from a Range Rover across the street. Had he been following them? Maybe not. As he closed his car door, an object fell from his pocket, a three-inch-long transparent cylinder. He picked it off the tarmac and slid it up his coat sleeve, then hurried to the phone booth a block away.

Quite mysterious for a gardener. Eileen was at the point of asking Rowena why a landscaper should carry test tubes when she stopped herself. Remember, it was Temple who made nice with Lady R. Got you in the castle garden. Don't go squealing right away, she figured. Wait at least until there's something in that tube.

Rowena led the way under the Wharf's wooden sign and into the dim interior of the pub. The pub interior looked dirtier than the street outside, like everything, from the seat cushions to the face of the barman had been rubbed with coal tar. The tables and chairs were built from thick black-stained wood that shone with age. The carpet, once a red floral, had matted from the constant traffic. Low-slung nautical lamps hung from the ceiling and provided enough light to identify faces but find no faults.

Several animated dart tournaments were under way a few steps from the lobby. A handful of middle-agers were gathered at the board, one cursing his score and two others slapping each other on the back. Everyone wore coveralls. Some zipped up, some undone, some yawning at the waist, sleeves dangling like drowned corpses. An old man with taped glasses stared openmouthed at Eileen. He poked his neighbor with the neck of his Newcastle, sloshing its contents on a nearby table. The friend turned to face Eileen, too. He was missing an arm.

With a rush of light, a college-age girl appeared through a swinging door to the kitchen. She looked about nineteen and wore a short red kilt and Doc Martins. The door swung shut behind her, extinguishing the brief light, and the pub resumed its ghoulish atmosphere. The waitress had a mermaid tattoo on her shoulder and, to Eileen's surprise, movie-star teeth.

"Sit where you like," she greeted Rowena. "Menu's on the board." A blackboard above the bar listed dinner choices in a schoolboy's script.

"I don't know how welcome we are here." Eileen sat at the one remaining table near the rear of the pub. Three men at the neighboring table turned their backs. "Poms," Eileen heard one of them say.

"Do we have to stay?"

"Don't let those wretches bother you." She glared at the one who made the "Poms" remark. "That's just Bruce *the Ruth* having a go at 'Who's better.' He and his mates come in here every night, throw eight or ten pints back, and try to out-Rutherford each other. They're jobless, so they bad-mouth visitors."

"What'll you have, then?" the waitress asked, her mermaid dancing as she made notations with a pencil. "Bruce," she added, "you botherin' the ladies?"

"He's irrelevant," Rowena answered. Bruce took a long drag on his cigarette, turned to Eileen, and blew smoke directly at her.

Rowena reached over to Bruce's table, took his pint of ale from under his nose, and poured in the contents of their ashtray ash tray. Bruce cursed a blue streak. The barman, Eileen guessed, had had enough. A fellow in a half apron jumped over his swing door and yanked him to the back room. A cheer went up from the tables, and Rowena took a bow.

Smiling broadly, Eileen ordered her food. She might enjoy the ale-house after all.

"Well, if it ain't the Yank!" came a voice from a corner of the pub. "What brings you to see the townies?"

Eileen looked up from her plate. The light was very dim, but she made out a young man in a Stones T-shirt and work boots, two-day stubble, and a long scar on his forehead.

"Hello, Hugh," Eileen murmured.

"We're here to introduce Eileen to fish-and-chips," Rowena said.

"Darla, love!" Hugh slurred at the pretty waitress. "Chips, extra portion, on the double!"

How had Hugh gotten so drunk so fast? They'd just seen him in the bull's paddock, sober. Maybe he carried a hip flask with him.

"I've been wantin' to talk to yis. You got space at yer table for a filthy farm lad?" He pulled at the legs of his coveralls, stumbled, and caught himself on the edge of a table. Eileen shifted in her seat and studied her hands. There were small flecks of polish still there from Chicago.

"Well..." Rowena started. "You bring the rest of the family, Hugh?"

"I'm with me girl Darla." He slapped the back side of the waitress. She'd been taking the order of the adjoining table.

"Hugh!" She scowled. "Behave."

"Och, you love it, lass!" To Eileen's horror, he sat down next to her and draped an arm across her shoulders. "Now, Eileen. How 'bout you tell me all about the US of A. You know, hip-hop, sock hops, roulette, and slots. Whatever it is you Yanks get up to in Sillinois."

"Illinois." Eileen squirmed out of the way. He smelled worse than a Midwest ethanol plant.

"Oh, so you're good enough for Ewan but won't take the time for the low-caste brother?" Spittle flew from his mouth.

"Young man," Rowena said, "should I send for the management?"

Hugh ignored her. He raised his mug as for a speech. Eileen covered her eyes. But before Hugh could speak, Ewan walked briskly over from the back room. He looked calm and purposeful and more intense than Eileen had ever seen.

"Right then. Let's get you home, old man." He hoisted his brother out of his seat and aimed him at the door. "Temple must have slipped him something. I'm sorry. He doesn't do this on a few pints."

"But the Yank!" Hugh waved his finger at Eileen. "She and those Poms need to know they're not welcome."

"I think he's made that pretty clear," Rowena whispered.

The two men staggered to the door, Hugh waving his arms and shouting, Ewan murmuring in his ear. And then Hugh took a swing at his brother. It was a lousy shot, but the violence of it knocked Hugh into an even bigger man standing at the bar. Ewan grabbed his brother by the collar then and half escorted, half dragged him toward the door.

"Just who do you think you are, goddamn it?" Spit flew in Ewan's face. "Just cuz you're her favorite doesn't make you my keeper."

"Tighten the leash, Stalker," came a voice from the shadows of the bar. Jenkins sat by himself on a bar stool. "Never know what a man's capable of when provoked, right, Ewan?"

"That man," Eileen whispered to Rowena. "He's the one who threatened me on the hillside."

"Nonsense." Rowena lifted a pacifying hand. "The man's a borrowed shirt. You have plenty of those back home, right? The Busboys of Bel Air?"

"*Housewives* of Beverly Hills."

"Housewife." Rowena nudged Eileen's elbow. "Fit title for Jenkins, eh?"

Eileen wasn't so sure. Both Ewan and Hugh had changed visibly when they saw him. Hugh's neck veins all stood up, and Ewan looked like he might chew the neck off his larger bottle.

However Jenkins seemed to like the impression he cast. He curled an arm around his teacup. Then when he and Ewan finally made eye contact, a curl came to his lip. "Watch that drunk of a brother. Wouldn't want to risk your tenancy." He recrossed his legs on his bar stool and returned the pages of *Horse & Hound*.

"You don't govern us, yet," Ewan growled. But Jenkins didn't look up from his magazine.

Eileen and Rowena finished their fish, though it was a hard dish to swallow. Not only had Hugh been publicly shamed with his display at their table, he'd been insulted by a servant of the castle. In front of her. This would do nothing to improve Hugh's attitude toward her, and it put Ewan so firmly at the crosshairs of factions, how would she ever get alone with him again?

As Rowena was paying their bill, Mr. Temple appeared through the curtain-draped back room, where Eileen had heard the thwack of the pool cue. He was stuffing a wad of pound notes in his pocket. A gambler? Bookie? If he was like the rest of the castle dwellers, he'd have his hand in many fires.

"Hugh go off this way?" Temple asked, scanning the tables. "I was trying to count his drinks," he said directly to Eileen. "Lost track during the skittles." He wiped a handkerchief across his face.

Eileen narrowed her eyes. Whatever skittles was, it clearly wasn't sweet-tart candy.

"They stumbled into the street." Rowena pointed the way. "Better see that your mate has a lift. Ewan's on his bike 'sfar as I can tell."

"Temple!" An angry voice came from the back room. A kilted man tore through the doorway a moment later. "You dropped your knave, mate. The one you had taped to your boot." The loud man hurled the playing card on the floor. There was a sound of applause from a distance and the clink of tankards. "Don't come in here again, you hear me? We know where you keep those wee porcelains."

Temple reddened a little and smoothed his shirtfront and shrugged his shoulders. Then he opened the bar door and disappeared. Conversation resumed. Bruce the Ruth told a joke about somebody's mother, and a Gaelic song started up on the jukebox. Rowena clapped her hands together. "Fabulous song." She rose and approached the jukebox to sing along.

Eileen was alone at the table. She could go try to find Ewan, follow him home. Was that desperate? Dangerous? Even if it was, she was tired of waiting on invitations. Back home, she was so cautious, she wound up most times being overlooked. Even spoiled Monica tried to coach her to increase her presence at school. *If you see a chance,* she'd say, *take it. Never slide under the radar.*

So...follow Ewan. Make him notice.

She hopped from her chair and tapped Rowena's shoulder. "I think I'll find a cab. I'm ready to go."

"Oh no! No darts? No sweets? There's bubble and spit."

"Box it for me."

"There won't be any cabs." Ewan's voice floated over the crowd.

She hadn't seen him come back in. Her mouth curled very slightly at the edge.

"Well..." Ewan rubbed his chin. "The nearest cab company's in Kirkcaldy."

"OK." Why did everyone like to contradict the American? Was it just that she was foreign, or a girl, or sixteen? He wasn't any older than she was. But he always got to be right. "I'll walk, then."

Rowena shrugged and grabbed another pint from the barman, then nudged her way among the dart players.

"Row!" someone said warmly. "You're on my team."

That Rowena—she'd make friends with a scorpion if it would sit down for a pint. Poor Granny, though. How was she going to manage these louts?

Eileen pushed the front door open, and Ewan quietly followed.

Outside the Wharf, she inhaled a mouthful of air and exhaled deeply. Though it was cold out, the sea air was a nice change from murky pub. The air still smelled of coal, but it was better than second hand smoke.

Some of these Scots had choices, though. They just didn't act on them.

It was dark out. A scattering of streetlights marked the road out of Leven, but there were no waiting cabs. No one at all. She really might end up walking. Oh, but there, a dome light came on. Must be a cab. She stepped off the curb and waved.

"Careful there." Ewan, behind her. Secretly, again. "You got to watch for traffic on the right here. It's not like in Chicago."

He was looking hopefully at her from the Wharf's doorway. In his green all-weather coat, he looked like a mythological green man, an environmental activist or rural do-good. Quick with the advice.

He looked down when she didn't react. "That's just Eric Montrose. In the car. He got the cop light for a laugh, but he's not a cabbie."

"You know, Ewan." Keep it polite. Don't offend him. "If I wanted help, I'd ask for it." She smiled curtly at that, took a few paces toward the car, and then watched it speed out of sight.

Damn. Why did he have to be right about everything? Yes, she liked this guy. Yes, he was charming. But his 24 hour expert feature wasn't so great. She turned on her heel looking for street signs. The one nearby lamppost had a directional marker reading *Rutherford Estate*, pointing east, into forbidding darkness. She nodded, stuffed her hands into her pockets, and strode forward.

Ewan's footsteps followed. He began to whistle. "So, would you consider some company?"

She made a half turn toward him. Those freckles, man! And the dark eyes, so, what?...hopeful. You'd never have guessed this teenager had just dragged his drunken brother out of a bar to avoid a fight. And even after that, he had no resentment about him. No annoyance, like she did. No why-is-it-always-me?

Eileen clicked her teeth, considering. What would Monica...Wait, she didn't care. There was no Monica. Not in Leven, not in the whole U.K. Eileen exhaled slowly and made a short nod, allowing Ewan to follow her down the dark road.

"I've never been much of a lad," Ewan said a few paces later.

She'd been wondering how to make conversation on a creepy road. The obvious topics—unemployment and alcoholism—being just too awful. But she'd never heard of "a lad."

"A player, you call it? My brothers are. And Hugh's a complete git when he's on the bottle. But he regrets it later."

"He really scared me back there."

"I'm sorry. I'd have stepped in earlier only I didn't know if you'd... Some girls don't like...rescuing."

"Well a 'how you been?' would be nice. You know, since you were there anyway." She touched the edge of her phone where it rested in her pocket. "And you never called me, after we exchanged numbers."

"I don't like mobile phones. And I'm here now."

Yes, he was. But was he making fun? "OK, but look. Something happened between us. At the cave you kind of...shut down. Remember? Was it because of the writing on the ceiling?"

He looked away, up the street. Then he lifted Eileen's hand, brought her knuckles to his mouth, and kissed them. "Does it matter?"

Eileen chest thumped. "I just wondered 'cause it seemed to upset you."

He kissed her mouth then. His approach caught her totally off guard, and she stumbled slightly. He caught her, though, and held her against him. His mouth was soft and purposeful, his lips calm, curious. He tasted like salt water, and his chin stubble tickled her nose.

When they parted, Eileen's eyes were searching. It had been a chaste kiss, sweet, and closed-mouthed. It had been present in her mind for so long, though, that the fact of it was more than she could really believe.

"Did you just kiss me?"

"I did." He laughed.

"I liked it."

He gave her hand a squeeze. They resumed walking. Eileen supposed they were only a mile from the estate, but the light on the narrow sidewalk was very poor. It was probably dangerous to be on the road at ten o'clock, on the slim walkway that got almost swallowed by seven-foot hedgerows. There'd been no streetlights since Leven, and the two driving lanes there'd been in town had merged to one, and there was no reflective paint to speak of. How did drivers see at night?

"I wouldn't like this walk alone," Eileen murmured. She was glad to be approaching the estate. No one drove at all on those roads, except for Clyde with the town car. And there was no stink of coal up there, the houses being heated by radiator, not coal.

"It's true, you shouldn't walk this route at night. Unless I'm with you." He wrapped an arm around her. As he did so, a pale fluorescent light flicked on a few yards ahead. In what had been a blacked-out storefront, a late-night diner appeared. They peered into the greasy window. A middle-aged man stood at the counter in a disposable apron. He was setting up menus and wiping down tables. A slogan was stenciled across the window: *Don't Go Leven Without Your Chips.*

"Should we go in?" Ewan asked.

They ordered two plates of cod and chips even though Eileen had already had the same thing back at the Plow. Ewan hadn't eaten and was ravenous.

As he ate his cod, Eileen foraged for conversation. "I met Lady Rutherford the other day."

"Did you, now? Can I?" He pointed to her fries.

She nodded.

"Hand me the vinegar?"

She did so, and Ewan wolfed her chips.

"Mr. Temple took me to the walled garden. I didn't really want to go at first, but I did, and it's gorgeous by the way. And that's where I saw your grandmother, pruning roses."

"Did she speak to you?"

"She did, and she took me on a tour. She showed me all her flowers and the chapel and..."

"The cemetery?"

"Yeah. That too."

Ewan considered this.

Eileen took a forkful of the remaining cod. It was delicious.

"Did you see Emily's headstone?"

She nodded. "Do you mind?"

"No." He reached across the table and curled a lock of Eileen's hair behind her ear.

She looked at her plate. "You could have told me earlier about your mother. And her accident."

"How'd you hear about it, then?" He wiped his mouth and folded his napkin.

"Rowena. But since we're friends, I'd hoped I'd hear it from you."

He turned away. "It's not a happy story to tell."

"I know, Ewan. I'm so sorry you lost her."

Twelve

The waiter cleared their plates. "Interest you in somethin' else, miss?"

"Two teas," Ewan suggested.

The chips man nodded and took their plates.

"Thanks. No. No milk for me." The tea was dark and bitter, but good.

"Emily's story," Ewan began. "It's not a big secret anymore." He took a sip of tea. The cup had a purple thistle on one side and *2007 Fife Games* emblazoned on the other. He set it down and rubbed the back of his neck. "When I was born, my mother, being a Rutherford, took me and me da to live in the Red House. Hugh was already seventeen and stayed on with Danny at the farm. They're his sons from an earlier marriage. Da ferried back and forth, sometimes with me and my mother, sometimes with my brothers. Lady Rutherford didn't want me around Hugh. He was, is, a bit course, to use her term. My da's first wife"—Ewan cast his eyes out the window—"Maureen, left him for the milkman. And it mighta' put ideas in his head. He did his own runner when I was twelve. He sent a postcard from the oil rig where he found work. But for the record, our da was a decent fella. Just restless. Made us grow up in a hurry, that's fir sure."

"By the time I was ten, though, there was no one left in Leven who knew how to farm. All the men wanted was to mine or drill oil. So after their mine went bust, the Rutherfords went close to bankrupt. But then our vet, Mr. MacDowell, got the laird interested in breeding. He trained me to tend the sheep on my summers, and he's also the one who sold Caedmon to us. He had already made good money as a sire when we

71

bought him. So my grandparents got Hugh trained up as a full-time handler. That sort of saved him. The husbandry job. He was no good in the mine, and his drinking had gotten bad. Tending the bull is good for him now. Keeps him stable, and it gets us headlines.

"Caedmon wins every show he enters. And he's easy work. Just lurks about his field and gets put out to stud a few times a year. He despises us, though, fenced in all by himself. Probably wishes us all dead."

Eileen took a sip of tea. "So your dad wasn't a bull handler, himself?"

Ewan shook his head. "He was sorta nervous around big animals. Didn't think they ought to be cooped up and certainly not used for stud. He preferred the free-range animals, like sheep. He always had his eye on the sea, though. No real wonder he ended up on a rig."

"When did Caedmon first charge someone?"

"Seven years ago. The first was the postman, poor bastard. The fog was so thick that day you couldn't see your hand in front of your face. The man took a shortcut through what he thought was an empty field. And in a dense fog, Caedmon just stands under his tree. Something got to him that day, though. A wasp sting, a sudden noise. God knows. But the postman got the worst of it. Gored in the shoulder right above the heart."

Eileen gasped. She'd seen a man trampled on a late-night cable show. But those were padded stuntmen riding doped steer for prize money. The Rutherford bull was the real thing. "Was he badly hurt?"

"Broke four ribs. Was in a body cast for ages. Lost half his spleen. And then there was my mother. Her accident wasn't bloody, at least. She took the same shortcut maybe, or someone accidentally left the lock unbolted on his gate. We'll never know. But somehow she and the bull were in the same field, and he charged."

"Awful," Eileen said.

"But no goring. She had a coronary. Caedmon never touched her. When the medics came, she'd been gone twenty minutes." He rubbed a finger across the edge of his teacup.

Eileen put her hand on Ewan's. How on earth did you console someone who'd lost both parents?

"She was buried in the ground where she was born. She and the Rutherfords had hardly spoken in years since marrying working class was such a breach. The laird still won't look at us Stalkers." Ewan took a deep breath. "Emily loved that walled garden. Before she met Da, she and Granny spent whole days up to their knees in dirt. Emily used to bury things around the estate—a game she played, like a squirrel. They were tiny things: a thimble, a wooden top, a makeup mirror. And she had a thing about opera gloves. She gardened in them. No work gloves. They had to be black satin opera gloves."

Eileen smiled.

"She made up this story," Ewan went on. "And Jenkins made her tell it all the time, about a treasure she'd found near the castle. Some ancient rune, Druid or Norse or whatnot. She called it a fortune stone and said she'd buried it and moved it around. Playing her game, yeah? Well, Jenkins bought it, even though she'd laugh at him tearing holes in the earth. 'Oi, Jenkins!' she'd say. 'Find your rune?' Made him blush down to his elbows. But he and Temple got completely wrapped up with it. I saw the two a' them digging a few times at night. Looked balmy, like a coupla' pirates."

"Why do you call your mother by her first name?"

"Emily was who she was. 'Mum' didn't really fit. She had a tattoo on her shoulder, of the Rutherford hare. She played guitar and went to concerts. She was just, you know, Emily." He looked at his watch and showed it to Eileen. Eleven forty. "I'd better walk you home."

They left the "chippie" and began the quarter mile back to the estate. The wind blew a low whistle through the hedgerows, and Eileen heard cows foraging on their other side. She flinched at the sound but Ewan didn't seem to have noticed. She wished he'd take her hand again.

"If the bull's so dangerous, why does your family keep him?"

"He's a thoroughbred," Ewan answered, and pushed a clump of gorse out of their path. "He makes the estate more money than the dairy, the barley, and the sheep put together. And he's so shot full of dope he's no danger anymore, since Hugh found the right tranquilizer. Caedmon saved them both, in a way."

"So"—Eileen nodded—"Hugh needs the bull."

"The bull was causing accidents, Hugh was becoming a career drunk. Then they found each other. Now Caedmon's doped stupid but he's not a risk to anyone, and he keeps Hugh too busy to drink. Mostly."

Eileen made a face. "Except for slipups like tonight."

"I know. And I also know he makes you uncomfortable."

"The bull or your brother?" They had reached the farm and were nearly at Ewan's doorstep. The porch light cast halos around their heads.

"You don't like either, do you?" Ewan lifted her hair from her shoulder and stroked it down her back, then placed a tiny kiss on her shoulder. "Rough as they are," he breathed into her hair, "We need them."

Thirteen

That night Emily paid Eileen a visit. Somewhere in the afterglow of Ewan's kiss and the deadweight of night's still hours, a rope found its way to Eileen's bedroom where it strung itself across the hardwood floor. It curled around the foot of her bed and trailed over the window, down to the ground below. At two a.m. Eileen felt a tug, like she was being pulled onto a moving train. But there was not train, just the urgency to get up and out of bed. Her blankets fell to the floor. There was more pulling, like an ocean current—soft yet powerful. She followed the guide rope to her window frame and peered after it, down the side of the exterior wall.

Ewan waited in the distance. His silhouette stood amid the waving barley on top of the hill where they'd first met.

"I'm coming!" she called, lowering herself down.

Ewan had Charlie on the leash. He waited obediently at Ewan's side.

She reached the ground and began to walk toward the hill. But she heard a roar. She turned slowly and saw where the noise had come from. It was Caedmon. He was charging at her from the castle.

Eileen stood motionless, anchored by some eerie magnetism to the Red House yard. Hooves thundered. Eileen lifted her arms overhead, and just at the point of collision, her dream shifted.

She was alone at the top of a cliff looking out at the Firth of Forth Bay. Her anorak was wrapped tight, but vicious wind flapped her hood around her neck. Though it was daytime, the sky coal gray, the sun barely penetrating angry clouds. Eileen's gaze focused on a cluster of figures twenty yards from her on the same stretch of cliff. It was three males, an old man in a kilt, a young man in a long rain slicker, and a boy of about nine. He clung to the young man, who was shouting.

"I will not put him down," the young man yelled. "I raised that animal. You're goona have to do it yourself."

"You'll do as I say on my farm!" The old man approached him. "He's dangerous!"

It was Lord Rutherford in the kilt. But here, he was upright. Walking, even. But he had something underneath his coat. A rifle!

"I am the lord here, Stalker." His face looked hard enough to break stones.

The younger man was clearly Hugh. But he stood straighter than Eileen remembered. His face was different. Smoother. Not the scabby wreck she'd seen at the pub. To look at Hugh here, he looked quite dashing. The boy who clung to him was Ewan.

Seeing Rutherford's rifle, Ewan let out a wail.

"Ewan, you come away, now," the old man commanded

"I won't!" Ewan voice cracked. "He's my brother. Don't point that gun at him!"

"Ewan! Mind your elders!" Lord Rutherford reached for the boy, but a gust shook him off balance. He flapped his arms to regain his footing, the gun waiving wildly in the air.

"Don't hurt him!" Ewan leaped at the lord.

They tussled, the boy and old man, staggering back and forth at the edge of the bluff. Somehow Ewan's hands got to the rifle.

"Look out!" she screamed from her spot on the cliff.

But her warning disappeared in the explosion. Ewan threw the smoldering gun to the ground. But too late. Hugh rolled over in the grass, blood pouring from his head.

Ewan threw himself on top of his brother, sobbing.

The old man tried to tear Ewan away, but he wouldn't be moved. He clung, kicking and screaming "murderer." A smart kick to the stomach finally ended their brawl. Ewan's boot caught the old man square in the gut. He staggered, pinwheeled, and fell soundlessly over the cliff.

Eileen woke on the floor beside her bed, blankets everywhere.

Then she ran to the window and drew back the curtain. She yanked the pane upward, searching vainly for Ewan, and vomited last night's fish-and-chips.

In the bathroom, where she went to rinse her mouth, something caught Eileen's eye out the porthole window, in the kitchen flower beds. It was a woman. From Leven? A friend of the Stalkers? She was moving among the flowers and...counting them? Identifying them? It had to be *Emily*! Yes, visiting her old garden. And, yes, she was singing "Speed Bonnie Boat." Eileen's stomach spasmed again. No more fish-and-chips. Was she still in that dream? She swallowed hard and opened the window for a better view.

Somewhere in the house, in the downstairs corridor maybe, she heard laughter. And running water in the kitchen.

"Charlie?" Eileen whispered.

No bark, though. No happy panting. More laughter. Then the tinkle of the music box. This time, the sound came from the stairs.

Suddenly Eileen's phone rang. She almost shrieked from her surprise. But it wasn't coming from her pocket, or her bedroom, but from downstairs or maybe even outside in the yard. She distinctly remembered putting the iPhone on its charger. And the ringtone she was hearing was a U2 song that she'd never downloaded.

She grabbed her coat and boots from the hallway closet. She was finding that phone. No one, be it ghost or dementor, messed with a person's iPhone.

The stairs were creaky and cold. She ran her fingers over the wall corners and crevices to help navigate the hallway. Then to the landing and the kitchen below. The phone had stopped ringing. On the coat tree in the foyer, she went through every raincoat, a parka, and Rowena's Peruvian poncho. No phone, but there was a wet French fry and half a crumpet.

U2 sounded again outside. What game was this ghost up to? No wonder Andrew Temple lost it. Eileen opened the door, though it made a horrible groan, and closed it as softly as possible. The cold was nearly shocking on her bare feet. Why hadn't she grabbed her shoes?

Now the phone was playing "Speed Bonnie Boat." How did you possess a phone like that? It was not just the notes this time. Along with the music an alto voice sang a verse Eileen had never heard.

Loud the winds howl, loud the waves roar
Thunderclouds rend the air;
Baffled our foes stand on the shore
Follow they will not dare

The voice stilled and a dot of neon lit the yard. Her iPhone, in the hands of a young woman. Emily. The ghost was a redhead not much bigger than Eileen. She wore a white concert T-shirt and beckoned with a black-gloved hand.

She wouldn't be unkind, surely, this, the mother of a boy they both loved. Her face looked gentle. But Eileen was afraid. She moved her feet three paces but no more.

"What do you want?"

The ghost disappeared. A breeze stroked the barley, and a bird called, then another farther off. Emily appeared again in the middle of the driveway, a white blur this time, pale against dark pebbles. She moved toward Eileen now. Her T-shirt came into focus. U2 Unforgettable Fire.

She moved like candle flame, flit and quiver, eyes darting, her feet a blur of silent motion. She seemed calm but moved with purpose. And she was elegant despite her Goth T-shirt and army boots. She could pass for a teenager if it weren't for her long opera gloves, strange even on a ghost. She didn't appear in her entirety as she swept over the Red House yard. Her torso, alone, was visible at first, then a single shoulder, then a leg, then the boots. And as she moved closer, she made a noise like "hushshshshshsh." She reached with one gloved hand and took hold of Eileen's arm.

"Help me," she whispered.

Nausea clutched Eileen's stomach again. She struggled to separate from the ghost whose grip on her shoulder was vice-tight and whose fingers, though gloved, were aching cold.

So she couldn't move, but don't panic, she reasoned. This was Ewan's mother. If she was anything like him, she would never hurt her. "How do I...help you, ma'am?"

She let Eileen's arm drop. "There's a boy on the farm. *He* needs your help, Eileen. Restore what's his."

"Ewan. What has he lost?"

The spirit lifted her hands to her face. "Mother doesn't want me to say." She let her arms drop back down and peeked through the shrubs toward the castle, a lot like Eileen had done the first two weeks on the estate. "The monster's loose."

"What monster?" But Eileen was pretty sure she knew.

"The great champion." Emily sighed. "Keep my boy safe from them and do what I couldn't. Restore what's his." She stepped backward into the hedgerow at that, and then there was nothing but Eileen's nervous breath dissolving into air.

Though tempted to chase after her, Eileen knew she couldn't follow. In the place where she'd been standing lay the iPhone. Streaming across the display were the lyrics she'd been singing plus the addition of an extra line. "Follow the syringe."

Fourteen

Despite the specter of the night, day dawned pink and shiny, almost as cheerful as an Evanston summer. Eileen helped Fran fold linens and tucked them into a cabinet that had just arrived on a truck from England.

"You might like this one." Granny stroked the surface of a comforter. It was small, for a child's bed, but lovely. Gold satin with a wildflower pattern in violet thread. "I had this made for your mother when she was your age. Maybe you'd like it for your own daughter one day." She winked.

Eileen ran her own hand over the blanket. It was smooth and cold and had a slight odor of mildew. "Granny?"

"Yes, darling?"

"Last night there was..."

"Come on, old lady. You can tell your one and only gran."

"OK." She folded the comforter and placed it in the armoire. "Well, you know at night, after everyone's asleep, I've been hearing noises. Running water. Music. And sometimes floorboards creaking..." She trailed off.

"Did something scare you, child?" Granny took Eileen's hand and led her to a chair. They sat, Granny on an upholstered rocker, leaning in close. She'd always been like that—giving her complete attention when something was important, no matter how random.

"It didn't actually scare me until last night. When I saw something."

"Do you mean *someone*?"

Eileen nodded. "I think I saw a ghost." Eileen looked over her shoulder. If Rowena heard her talking about ghosts, she's split her pants laughing.

"The woman in evening gloves?"

Eileen's eyes widened. "You know about her?"

"The Rutherford ghost, yes. I've seen her, too. She's lurked around the Red House for years. You know, it's quite special to have an encounter with a spirit. Most people are too closed off. But"—Granny winked—"your Scottish blood, it allows you to see special things. I've seen spirits. Well, one." She nodded with satisfaction. "Your grandfather visited me after his death. Our family's special that way, so it doesn't surprise me that Emily likes you. When I saw her, she was in the vegetable garden digging for something, in opera gloves! The same spot that mad Jenkins likes to turn over. Anyway, it was just the one time, and she didn't speak."

"I didn't know Jenkins went through our garden." Eileen did see him ankle deep in a hole by the greenhouse the day she met Lady Rutherford, but never at the Red House.

"Oh, yes. He digs everywhere. A regular groundhog. Maybe he lost his favorite tie pin. He was at it just a few nights ago. Don't 'spose he found more than radish seeds. And he didn't even warn me he'd be unearthing my vegetables."

"Well, last night Emily *did* speak to me. She knew who I was, too."

Granny leaned in closer. "What did she say?"

"She wanted me to find a boy and restore something to him. And she was afraid of some monster."

Granny glanced out the living room window at the castle, then squeezed Eileen's hand. "I'm sure that gave you a fright."

Granny leaned back in her rocker, a faraway look on her face. "Let's just keep this to ourselves, for now."

"You don't think I need to do something, though?" Eileen replied. "She seemed upset."

"You don't know *what* she wants restored, right? It could be jewels or a team of horses, something really hard to get your hands on. If I were you, until she tells you specifically what you should restore, wait. Taking part in the affairs of the dead is tricky. When your grandfather's ghost came 'round, he just wanted to sing jazz tunes. Wait until Emily asks for something concrete."

Fifteen

The Red House garden progressed nicely. Eileen went out every morning to water and weed. She planted several flowering bushes: lilac, hawthorn, a small rhododendron. It was hard work digging, removing stones, hauling soil and gravel. Eileen discovered she enjoyed turning featureless turf into flower beds. Preparing a Dairy Queen blizzard last summer wasn't half as satisfying.

Charlie interfered, of course. He dug up Joyce's beets and half the rhododendron. At least that's what Mr. Jenkins claimed when he came by to take a look at their progress. Though Granny was the only one who saw him, the strange little man continued to sneak over in the dark with his spade. Once he dropped his trowel on a fallen weathervane and woke Rowena. She put her head out the window with an "Oi, whatcherdoing, nosy!" She said he made like he had been chasing Charlie out of the vegetable beds, but Charlie was curled up at Rowena's feet.

"Clear off!" she shouted. "Or I'll hit you with my umbrella! My dog's no parsley vandal!"

They'd howled laughing.

The garden became Eileen's regular chore. At home, she mowed and raked their lawn, but they didn't have much space in Evanston for vegetables. And there were so many other distractions. Now that she'd embarked on the Red House garden, Eileen realized she liked it. It was her project, prompted by Granny but nevertheless her own. And she was good at it. The cool, gritty feel of loose earth was invigorating. Even the worms and beetles interested her. Especially since she spent a lot of time rescuing them from Charlie.

"That's a lot of dirt for a city girl."

Eileen stood up from a primrose bulb. Ewan was striding toward her across the driveway. She tugged off her work gloves and did her best to smother a grin. He looked quite different. More grow-up. Had he cut his hair? He'd always looked handsome and outdoorsy, like he belonged in a North Face commercial, but today he'd left the anorak and boots at home. He had a tweed jacket on over a burgundy turtleneck. On his feet were tidy loafers and, the biggest surprise of all, he wore a kilt.

"Going somewhere special, ma'am?" She grinned.

"It's me clan tartan." He bowed. "I thought I'd pop 'round to see if you'd fancy a trip to the games."

"You'll have to speak Pommy. I don't follow the Scotch."

"Yeah, little chance of that. You're Yank to the core. But since I like you, I'll translate. But I expect you to write down what I say and remember it for next time."

She saluted. "Roger."

"Right then. You've heard of the Highland Games?"

"Is that where you hurl a telephone pole?"

"That's the stuff." He winked. "Us clan folk like to toss the wee cabers and parade with swords in the family tartan. It's fair decent sport, especially for you tourists. So if you don't have too much more mud to fling on that poor spot of garden, can I be takin' you along?"

"You're on! Do I wear a kilt, too?"

"Do you have one?"

"I could probably find one in a trunk. Granny's half Scottish."

"Well, the kilts are more for the men folk at the games. Impresses the she-folk." On that, he stamped twice, causing his pleats to sway.

"Bravo, clan Stalker!" Rowena cheered from her golf chair under a tree.

"Give me five minutes." Eileen tossed her trowel in a bucket. "I'll just go scrape the dirt off."

After throwing on a sundress, Eileen actually beat Charlie down the stairs to join her date. A yellow truck had pulled up into the yard while she was changing, and Evan was leaning on its hood. Inside were both his brothers.

"Well, looks like the rest of the regiment's coming. You remember Hugh." Ewan indicated the truck's driver.

Crap. Brothers along on a date. What was the matter with them? And Hugh at the wheel. What Ewan put up with! It was a date! And she'd agreed to go, no matter how many brothers.

As she approached them, Hugh got down from his seat and came around to the passenger door, thumped it with his fist, and hauled it open. The hinge groaned deeply, but Eileen sat on the passenger side nonetheless, trying not to cringe as she slid a naked leg over the cracked vinyl. *How do I keep getting stuck with Hugh Stalker?* The elder brother barely looked at her, though. He banged the door shut and came around to the driver's seat. Maybe, in his silent, brooding way he was trying to make up for the night at the Wharf.

Ewan swung into the backseat along with the other guy, a teenager of about nineteen. "This is my other brother, Danny." He nodded at his seatmate. Eileen remembered him from the calving. He smiled and nodded. That was something, anyway.

Make nice, she coached herself. There was no reason to think Hugh would get out of control. They were going to the games was all. Just like family night at a Northwestern football game. Good, old-fashioned fun.

"I remember you, Danny, from that day at the barn."

"This your first games?" Hugh pulled onto the road to Leven. He was paler-looking close-up than Eileen remembered. Worry lines creased the corner of his mouth, and the eyebrow scar looked crueler than ever.

"Well, my mom and I did some Scottish dancing at 4-H. We have Scottish blood. But our club didn't have much Highland to it. We practiced in a Big Lots cafeteria."

"Well, Ewan here will show ye a good time." Hugh reached over the seat back and cuffed Ewan on the chin. "He's a one with the ladies!"

"Hugh." Ewan narrowed his eyes.

"What? I was gonna say that you're a gentleman, and not 'alf bad at the sword dance. Or were you gonna toss the caber today?" Hugh smiled broadly and lurched the truck into third gear.

He didn't look much like Ewan. Eileen guessed he was about twenty-eight, but his face and hands were weathered like someone twice his age. His fingers, where they gripped the wheel, were gnarled like old tree roots. Farmwork must have really taken a toll on the fingers. His looked like red-skinned potatoes. Danny was a little more like Ewan—but only in the chin. Ewan must favor his mother.

In his features, there was something unearthly, a brow he'd borrowed from a fox, the eyes from a harbor seal. They were dark blue-gray and searching. Always. They concentrated, too, without blinking. And yet, despite his intensity, he face was uniquely alive. His hands were in constant movement, flicking a stone, tossing a coin, whittling. Though the fingers were worked like his brothers', his were not the brutish knuckles that gripped the pickup's wheel. They were more like gently warn leather. Something you'd like to touch and smell. Often.

"You really dance with swords, Ewan?" Eileen swiveled to face the backseat.

"And he plays the pipes!" Danny added.

"He thinks he can tame old Caedmon with that bagpipe." Hugh leaned toward Eileen. She moved her arm so it wasn't so close to his. "Scotts first made the pipes to scare their enemies. But the way this fella plays 'em, he'd charm the horns off the bull!"

Ewan reached over the seat back and smacked his brother in the head.

They arrived a half hour later to a farm a few fields smaller than the Rutherfords'. One pasture, mowed short for the festival, was designated for event parking, and two others were roped off for competition, with bright orange yardage lines spray-painted on the turf. Rental tents stood at the intersection of two dirt roads. Inside, locals sold wooden toys, tartan blankets, coats of arms, heraldry signs, beer steins, walking sticks, and imitation throwing cabers.

"Hey, that tent's your granny's." Eileen pointed at a luxurious marquee. In fact, it was the largest pavilion at the games, a *Rutherford* signature emblazoned across the top in a golden script. Banners blew from the top of the marquee and the family tartan, in wide bands of blue and black, blazed on an A-frame placard at the entrance. It was the same tartan that Ewan wore today, in fact.

Ewan led her to the entrance, but Eileen kept back a pace, eyeing the tartan inside.

"You sure?"

He shook his head at her and towed her in after him.

Though the tent was expensive, the interior of the pavilion was a lot more down-to-earth. Like a tailgate party back home. Gaelic crosses hung on portable jewelry displays. Visitors charted their branch of the Rutherford family on a large, table-mounted history. You could buy a coat of arms on a brass or pewter shield or get your silverware engraved with the Rutherfords' patrimonial bull symbol, two horns entwined with barley stalks.

Next to the coats of arms perched a glass case filled with daggers made of brass, silver, treated lead. Some were delicate, nearly elvish, and others were as long as Eileen's arm and sharp enough to skewer an ox. They were sold with holsters, fanny packs, scabbards; one pack was tooled to look like the head of a unicorn, the blade sticking out of the animal's forehead. A mob of some eighty people were in there, all of them men, all wearing Rutherford tartan and shouldering their way to the checkout lane.

She tried to remember if she'd seen these faces in town. None looked familiar. "Why are these people here, exactly?"

"Och, you know. Pissing contest." A hurried man sidestepped past, jostling Eileen. Ewan placed his palm on her back. A warmth spiraled upward from the center of his hand. "They show off their kilts and out-Rutherford each other, see who's the next laird. Then they get drunk and punch each other's lights out. There's some dispute over who's the official heir, so..."

"Aren't you—"

"Look." He pulled her out of the marquee, cutting her off. "Can't miss the buffet tent."

They neared a case of sugared baked goods, and Ewan spoke close to Eileen's ear. "Granny doesn't like us to have the peerage conversation in public." They both looked back the way they'd come.

"You mean in front of those...fans?"

Ewan nodded and pointed with his chin. "Prime example right there." A middle-aged guy in a "Dundee" T-shirt had his finger in another man's chest.

Being out-classed back home in Evanston was pretty ordinary. Some teenagers she knew drove Humvees while others at the same school barely kept their winter coats done up with safety pins. But in Ewan's case, pretending to be someone you weren't, in a country where it really mattered, that must be just awful.

Ewan grabbed her hand. "Can't leave Scotland without having a scone."

Inside the buffet tent, a couple of busty women in medieval dress poured beer, and younger girls with higher collars took charge of tea. Scones came around on trays along with hot cross buns, crumpets, and something called *spotted dick*.

Ewan laughed at her look of horror. "It's just custard."

Eileen blushed. She hoped the culture difference would even out soon. Too many things shocked her still. How nice it would be to have Ewan's ease with the world, though it had cost him.

He paid for the pastries, and they ate them at a wooden picnic table in the buffet tent. The pastry was smaller than what you got at Starbucks and had no raisins or chocolate chips, but it was good in a buttery, baking-soda way.

A voice barked to life over the games' loudspeaker. "Ladies and gentlemen..."

"C'mon." Ewan grabbed her hand. "Sport's on."

Eileen tottered after him through the torn-up field. She cast one more look into the Rutherford family tent as they passed it, the would-be Rutherfords all lining up for a title. And she realized: *that* was what Emily had been talking about. The Rutherford *title* was what Ewan had lost! She wanted Emily to return it to him. His name and inheritance. But how was she supposed to do that with a crazy lord, a threatening butler, a rampaging bull, and a frenzy of wannabes duking it out for the very same thing?

"Over there." Ewan pointed to a set of bleachers.

They sat among the gathering fans, a wide field spread in front of them. Four men who had been weight lifting since infancy huddled on a bench at the games' edge. The contestants, Eileen figured. Each wore a muscle shirt and kilt.

"That tartan"—Ewan nodded to one of athletes who wore green-and-gray kilt—"can only be worn by a MacArthur. And that one by a Cameron. If you come to the Highland Games in someone else's kilt, you're likely to be thrown out. Or get a dirk at your throat."

"What's a dirk?"

"One 'a those daggers they buy as souvenirs. They're Scotch military regalia but used as parade-wear nowadays."

"So do Scots still fight with them?" She wondered if Hugh or any of the guys she'd seen at the Warf wore a dagger.

"No, these are collectibles and really blunt. And most of the fellas here are athletes. They spend all year training for this event."

Eileen liked to believe him, but his Scotland the Brave didn't seem to hold true in Leven, with all of two streetlights but a pubful of jobless drunks.

Ewan watched her, considering. "You saw the worst of things the other night at the Warf. It's not always like that."

"I know."

Ewan knit his hands together in his lap. "See that bloke over there?" He pointed to an athlete warming up with a deadly looking cycle. He had a shaved head and wore a yellow-and-gray kilt. "He's won the caber toss every year for five seasons. He goes to Australia and Canada and the States, wins every title. Then he comes home to his widowed da and helps him mend farm equipment. He has a pint like the rest of them, but he's not a yob."

"Great term, yob. I can name a few back home who could answer to that, though ours paint themselves purple and streak naked through parking lots on football Saturdays."

"Oi," Ewan tugged Eileen to her feet. "It's starting."

All around them, the people rose and removed their hats. Eileen expected something like "God Save the Queen" to play. She put her hand over her heart but, seeing no one do the same, dropped it back down. A low drone started somewhere out of view, and then, in a sort of accordion-harpsichord collision, it exploded in sound. By fours, an ensemble of bagpipers flowed their tartan river in front of the spectators. They marched in perfect formation, each man wearing red-white-and black kilts. Their costume included a cape of the same tartan slung over one shoulder and fastened with a silver brooch. Each had a tall furry hat, polished white spats, and a fanny pack on a chain around the hips. These weren't the cheap nylon numbers tourists wear in New York. Each was edged in animal fur, ermine, or sable or something. There must have been fifty pipers strutting in unison along the dirt road. And what a sound! Like an organ but more cheerful. Eileen immediately understood the importance of that kilt. It revealed the muscular legs of the wearer, and with every step, the pleats swung from side to side as the cape sailed out behind. They stood at attention for the final note, and the crowd roared. The games were on.

Ewan touched Eileen's elbow. "We can sit now. Here come the umpires."

Three green-jacketed men walked to the center of the game field and bowed to the crowd. Two wore a black-and-white tartan along with the regulation blazer. The other had a navy-blue-and-yellow kilt and, under his jacket, an Aerosmith T-shirt. "Ladies and gentlemen," the announcer started, "the caber toss."

"What exactly is the caber?" Eileen whispered.

"That." Ewan pointed to a seven-foot log on the ground. It was a tree trunk, pure and simple—seven feet tall and a half foot wide.

Who would turn that into sporting equipment? Eileen wondered.

"Back during the wars with the English," Ewan said, as though he'd heard her pondering, "when the Highlanders tried to put a Scotsman on the throne, the English stripped them of their weapons. They wanted to keep training but had to manage with objects they could scrounge: hay bales, farm equipment, bits of wood. So now we have the caber toss."

"Those are the judge." Ewan pointed at two of the green jackets who were conferring with each other at a painted yard line. "That one's the back judge, and the other's the side judge. They get two angles on the caber to see if it's thrown clean."

"How do you win?" Eileen watching the guy in the Aerosmith shirt stretch his shoulders. He had a chest like a refrigerator.

"A good throw turns the caber end over end and lands perpendicular to the thrower. Watch that bloke, Mark Shaw. He's smaller than some of the others but skilled. With the right grip, even a wee lad can make a good throw."

Shaw finished stretching and strode to the telephone pole. The log looked nine feet long, not seven, and at least three hundred pounds. The back judge approached the pole, picked up one end, and leaned it into the younger man's waiting arms.

"Shaw has to get a good grip now," Ewan explained, "or he'll drop it."

The man wrapped his hands around the back of the log and maneuvered his palms till they clutched the caber's underside. Grunting, he hoisted the pole straight into the air. The back judge hopped out of the way.

"How much does it weigh?" Eileen grabbed Ewan's knee. "Won't he hurt himself?"

"Shh!" someone said behind her.

"Don't worry," Ewan whispered. "Drops don't happen much at this level of competition."

Sure enough, this guy Shaw was no novice. He took just one wobbly step backward before he charged just three steps, nostrils flaring, and heaved the caber upward. Wonder if they watch bull's charge as practice, Eileen considered

Though Shaw's throw wasn't graceful, his log made a full ninety-degree turn and landed ten yards away. The audience cheered, and the referees ran to the impact site to take measurements.

"Was it a good toss?" Eileen asked.

"Hard to tell from where we're sitting. The judge wants a twelve o'clock." Ewan craned his neck for a better view. Many of the spectators were doing the same.

"Go, Shaw!" someone yelled from the first row of seats. "You done 'er!"

"A twelve o'clock? Is that a really straight throw?"

"It's the angle the caber lands at. You want it almost exactly parallel to the angle you started at. If you're off to one side or the other, a ten o'clock or a two o'clock, the score isn't as high."

"And if you drop it?"

"You'd get two more turns. Best of three's your score."

Shaw got an eleven o'clock and got his name entered on a board of ranked players.

Eileen and Ewan watched twelve more athletes compete, some young and buff, some still learning. Eileen cheered for the old guys and the skinny ones with fewer fans.

"Shall we go for a pint?" Ewan asked after the last competitor. "They serve a nice ale by the dance stage."

They took a pair of mugs from the barman and sat down on a wooden bench to watch the dancing competition that was beginning on the stage in front of them.

Seven gray-kilted men advanced to the stage. They were in what looked like very dressy tartan and each carried a sword. They took their places in a circle.

"Look, Ewan. Mr. Temple!" Ewan was tickling the chin of someone's border collie. "He sure gets around. I had no idea he was a dancer."

"There's more to these folks than you'd think. Those two blokes on either side of Temple, they were throwing darts at the Wharf that night. That one's Craig, and the other's his mate, Neil."

Eileen smiled at them. What a change from the surly guys in coveralls.

The loudspeaker came on again to announce the sword dance.

Offstage, a piper began their accompaniment, and the seven men began their dance. First they placed the flat of each sword on the shoulder of the man in front and danced a circle. Then they did figure eights, climbing over and slithering under each other's sabre. It was fast-paced. Every several steps one of the men yelled "ho" or "oh there," and the others whooped in reply. The next trick was for each man to take a turn climbing over the sword of the man in front of him while still marching in the circle. Then each dancer lifted his sword over his head and turned a circle underneath it, all while clasping the blade of the man behind him. After some fifteen dangerous-looking maneuvers, the dancers separated, each blade tip went up, and they trooped offstage.

The man on the loudspeaker cheered, "Let's hear it for the duffers, folks. Best dancers at the games. On a side note, Andrew Temple will be offering lessons to ladies who buy him a bottle of Newcastle."

Next, the stage turned over to younger dancers. There were scores of performers and tartans and argyle, athletes of all ages and fitness levels. It impressed Eileen, the inclusiveness of these events, where you could be an overweight old woman, a weird teenager, or a drunk, and still compete. It never worked like that back home.

Eileen's second ale was having its way with her, and after the third dance ensemble, she was on the verge of exploding. On her jog to the Porta Loos, she noticed a livestock competition finishing in the field across from the beer tent. Fifteen cows were standing at the end of lead ropes beside their handlers. The animals were all black and white with varieties of shaggy hair. They were getting the once-over from a man in a white lab coat carrying a clipboard. He examined the animals' heads and chests, took measurements, and ran his hands through tufts of hair.

It was a fast competition. By the time Eileen finished in the bathroom, a ribbon hung from the harness of a meaty creature by the fence. It was...was it?...it was Caedmon. And, yup, right at his shoulder, shaking hands with the judge, was Hugh. For the first time since she'd met the guy, he was smiling. He even stroked old Caedmon on his slab of neck. Eileen made a wide arc around a group of pipers to avoid Hugh's eye.

Caedmon began to stamp. And snort. He yanked hard at the lead rope. Hugh spoke quietly to him and tried to reassure him, touching his shoulder and side. But it was too late. A wicked tick had sprung to life.

The other handlers urged their animals off the field, and soon it was just Hugh and his increasingly agitated bull in the parade ring. Caedmon pawed the ground and swung his wooly head side to side. The judge who'd shaken Hugh's hand earlier approached him, carrying a stack of papers.

Eager to understand Caedmon's impulses, Eileen hid at the edge of the nearby tea pavilion.

"Mr. Stalker." The judge clutched the clipboard tightly.

"Yes, I'll get him out. He's not usually like this." But Caedmon was turning sharper and sharper circles around Hugh, his breath getting shorter and fiercer on each.

"Mr. Stalker! That animal's registration sample has just been flagged for steroids."

"What?" Hugh's arm went slack. "My sample cleared before the competition. How is it...?"

"Been tampered with? I don't know, son. But look at that animal. He's not normal. Check the blood work at St. Andrews if you like."

"Steroids?" Hugh yanked Caedmon's leash. The judge recoiled a little.

"You best cooperate, Stalker. The compound in his blood makes him dangerous. Get him stabled so he doesn't put anyone at risk."

"But don't you see? Someone's sabotaged me!" Hugh flung his arm out wide. "He was clean this morning, the vet came and took a sample himself. In front of me. Stop it!" he shouted at the prancing bull. "Calm down."

"We take unscheduled samples in your trailer now. I'm sorry, but this animal has failed the drug test. You can take it up with the county if you like, but I'll have to reclaim that rosette. And the check."

Hugh tore an envelope from his pocket and stuck it in the judge's face. Cursing, he led the snorting Caedmon away. He bucked twice and flung his head around, forcing Hugh to drop the lead rope and back away from a moment. After a few halfhearted charges at his shadow, Caedmon calmed down and followed Hugh to his trailer. Hugh was so red in the face as he left the field, Eileen wondered if she should warn the Newcastle Ale tent to close for half an hour while he cooled down.

Had Caedmon been sabotaged? Eileen wondered. He was calm and obedient 'til the rosette appeared on him. Then even the judge thought he'd lost it. And he probably saw some pissed off cows. Could Hugh have accidentally OD'd Caedmon? An error that big would cost his job. Even a drunk would know that.

Could it have been a rival owner in the competition? Another handler? The judge himself or the vet? In a region without steady work, most anyone might slip the bull a mickey for a price.

"You won't believe what just happened." Eileen waved Ewan over. He had her jacket and was preparing to leave. "I just passed the bull competition."

"Breeders Cup?" Ewan corrected.

"Right. Breeders Cup, which Caedmon won! But in the time it took me to use the loo, the bull completely lost it. Snorting, bucking, storming around the ring. The judge stripped the ribbon right off him."

Ewan's chin fell. "And the prize money. Oh, Hugh."

"Wait, it's worse. Hugh's mad as hell, too. He thinks someone sabotaged him cuz the reason they said they were taking back the prize wasn't just Caedmon's storming around the field. His blood sample came back positive for steroids."

"Shit. I'm sorry, Eileen. But shit. Hugh's gonna blow a gasket."

"What should we do? Can we go reason with the judge?"

Ewan turned to her with an eyebrow raised. He was about to speak when the feedback noise came on from the games' speakers. "Ladies and gentlemen, the top scores have now been calculated in the heavy games and dance competitions. It is our great fortune that Laird and Lady Rutherford will administer the honors."

Was Laird Rutherford here in the flesh? The man who never left the castle? The games seemed woefully working-class for him. But yes, there they were. Lady Rutherford wore her gray hair in a French twist along with a black kilt, wool blazer, and black gloves. Beside her was the man who must be her husband. In a wheelchair. Eileen had pictured him a silent and imposing man, a Prince Phillip type. But imposing he was not. The real man was shriveled and weak, leaning heavily to one side of his wheelchair, which pushed by Earnest Jenkins. Jenkins was in a business suit with his customary comb-over.

The laird had a black tartan blanket on his lap and an oxygen tube attached to his nose with a tank clamped to the side of his chair. If it wasn't for the tank, Eileen would have wondered if the man was breathing at all. He didn't blink. He didn't twitch. He just stared.

Eileen thought of Granny Fran. She'd aged a lot in the two years since Eileen had seen her. How many summers did these folks have left? Would Fran end up in a wheelchair? Eileen wished she'd never made a big deal about unpacking boxes or sent those spiteful texts to Monica about the elderly. It was unconscionable.

Lady Rutherford presented medals to the winners of the heavy events and highland dancing. Eileen stared at the laird meanwhile, waiting for a sign of life. A moth landed on his ear, though, and nothing. A jet passed overhead. Not even a blink.

"Did Lord Rutherford have a stroke?" Eileen asked at the end of the ceremony as she and Ewan made their way to the truck.

"That's what they say." He cleared his throat. "That's the first time I've seen him this year." He shrugged at Eileen's look of surprise.

"But he's your grandfather."

"And he still hasn't forgiven my mother. Not much to talk about with him, wheelchair or no."

"And what about that stooge?" Eileen nodded at Jenkins. "Why's he so tight with them?"

Ewan narrowed his eyes. "No one really knows Jenkins. He's a bullshitter and a show-off. But—" Ewan cut himself short. "Granny says he dotes on the old man, so...fine. At least the laird has a friend."

Weird, Eileen thought. She had never heard Ewan insult anyone. Jenkins must really be a toad. He had no title, had slunk into a coveted position at the side of a powerful man, and put on airs around the Stalkers like he was their lord and master. At the right moment, she'd have to ask how Ewan put up with it. How Lady R. did, too, who was still needle-sharp.

Jenkins was giving particular attention to settling his boss into the backseat of the Bentley. Lady Rutherford barely glanced at her husband. She chatted with Clyde while Jenkins buckled the old man in.

Eileen was about to slide into the yellow pickup they'd ridden in to the games, but Jenkins arrived suddenly at Ewan's elbow and gave him a pronounced *eh hem*.

"What is it, Jenkins?"

"You might want to track down your brother. Again. He's been cited for doping the lord's bull."

Ewan closed the door after Eileen. From her place in the front passenger seat, she could tell he was struggling with his reply. She lifted her hand and touched the window glass that separated them. He reached for hers, but before he made contact with the pane, he spoke. Slow and clear: "Be careful, Jenkins."

But the butler hadn't heard. Or else didn't care. That rope he was fraying apart would snap soon and sting fiercely when it did.

"Hugh must be keen to keep his job, with all the trouble he caused when your father first died. Why not do the bloke a favor." Jenkins leaned close to Ewan at that. Too close. "Tighten the leash."

"Put a lid on it, Jenkins," Ewan snarled. "Provoking him is a mistake."

"Threats, is it? Mmmm. I understand. You're a lad in a farmhouse who has to borrow another clan's kilt. Nice touch with the sporran there. I wouldn't bother with the Rutherford tartan much longer, though. Soon as the old man goes, rabble won't have the privilege."

"*You're* still a hired man." Ewan had colored in the last few minutes, and his breathing rate had increased visibly.

Eileen gripped her hands together. Should she step in? She played with the button of her cardigan. Shit, shit. Why was Jenkins winding Ewan up? Family conflict wasn't supposed to happen on a date!

Ewan took a few paces closer to Jenkins.

"No, Ewan," Eileen whispered.

"You may have pulled the wool over his eyes"—Ewan indicated the Bentley—"but the rest of us know your game. It'll be a cold day in hell before I answer to you."

Unbothered, Jenkins turned his attention to Eileen next. "Lovely lass there." A ball of saliva had gathered at the corner of his mouth. He looked more and more like a lizard all the time. "Keep your wits about you. People are known to have accidents around you."

Eileen's jaw dropped. He'd just threatened her! She went to open the door and give that righteous creep an earful, but the door was locked. From the outside! She worked on the handle, smacked at it. "Ewan!"

But he'd had the same idea Eileen had. "Bastard! You leave her alone." He took aim and cuffed Jenkins smartly on the chin. The man reeled backward, caught himself on the trunk of a Range Rover, and rubbed at his face.

Ewan squared off and shifted his weight from foot to the other. "Who do you think you are threatening people? Eileen's never bothered you, and she's a guest on my land."

"Ewan! Jenkins!" Lady Rutherford shouted from the far side of Bentley. She was slowly making her way out of the backseat and leaning on Clyde's arm. "What on earth's the matter?"

But Ewan wasn't waiting for permission anymore. His dignity had been challenged, much like Hugh's earlier. It wasn't coming back until he'd taken a few more shots. "Hugh's worked this farm all his life. He drinks, but no more than any other Scott. For God's sake, stop cowering, Jenkins. Stand up like a man."

But Jenkins did not stand up like a man.

"Lady Rutherford," he whined from behind the parked Range Rover. "Can you restrain this child!"

Ewan laughed cruelly. "Now you're getting an old lady to fight for you?"

"Ewan," Eileen murmured through her now lowered window. "That's enough."

"Not your fight, Eileen." He went around the side of the Range Rover and approached Jenkins from another angle.

The man shielded his head with his arms. "Call him off, call him off!"

Lady Rutherford shook Clyde away, standing to her full height and brandishing her walking stick. "Ewan Stalker, Earnest Jenkins. Stop behaving like animals!"

Ewan straightened, spat in Jenkins's direction, and returned to Eileen. "Sorry, Granny," he said as he passed Lady Rutherford.

She cuffed him gently on the shoulder. "You know better. Don't get yourself in such a strop."

"Well, he should know his place."

"And he shouldn't get to wear the tartan!" Jenkins shouted back.

"Shut up, parasite." He tried the driver's door of the yellow pickup then, but Eileen shook her head no. His eyes still burned. He looked like housecat enjoying the sight of a half-dead bird.

"I'm sorry, Eileen. I shouldn't have hit him, all right? But he was asking for it."

Silently, Eileen let herself out of the Stalkers' car and began walking toward the Leven road. She wasn't letting any of these men drive her in the state they were in. She'd walk, thank you, and be glad for it.

Though it was shocking to see Ewan's flare of anger, she was a little thrilled that he had a fighter in him after all. Someone rebellious beneath all that responsibility. He did have Emily inside him. She knew it. Too bad it took someone as pitiful as Jenkins to bring his passion out. How much better would it be if that strength and purpose went into kissing her again? Pushing her up against a barn door. Touching *her* eyes and mouth like he did with his grandfather's sheep.

Eileen nudged Ewan away from the Bentley. After just a few steps, his brother Dan caught up. "Not taking the lorry?" Behind him a few yards was the yellow truck with four disorderly men loading into the backseat. They were singing and passing a six-pack. A sheep dog Eileen didn't recognize bounced across the front seat.

Ewan raised his eyebrow. "Want to?"

"Six drunk guys in that car?" Eileen said. "I'd rather walk."

Ewan shrugged and Danny returned to his friends. "Oh," he called back to his brother. "Check with Hugh before you leave. Temple had to drag him out of the pub again."

Ewan groaned. "Jesus!"

"I'll go with you," Eileen said. "It's OK. You shouldn't have to take care of him alone all the time."

Back at the games' site, Hugh staggered down a row of chairs, most of them being cleared by festival staff, who avoided the reeling drunk as best they could. Then from up on the dais where the awards had been given, Temple emerged, his kilt and jacket in a dry cleaning bag. "Och, Hugh!" He stepped quickly to Hugh's side, grabbed hold of his shirtsleeve, and then half carried, half dragged him to a bright red mini.

"Oi, Temple," Ewan shouted from the edge of the parking lot. But Temple didn't hear them, or didn't wish to. He bundled Hugh into the car, opened his side, and took off.

"Is this a bad spat," Eileen asked Ewan, "or is he like this a lot?"

"Well, at the Sterling football game last year, he wound up in a water fountain."

"Does he ever listen to reason? If not to you, then to Temple or his doctor? You can kill yourself drinking like that."

"When me or Dan try to put it to him like that, he calls Danny a child. And me, I'm *just like the old man.*"

"Meaning your father or Lord Rutherford?"

"I don't know if he knows. He's sure I'm trying to run him out of the family. But I'm not. I'm just trying to keep peace. I should have tried for Clyde's job. No one ever yells at Clyde."

Sixteen

"So I see why you and Jenkins aren't friends, but a fist fight? Doesn't really seem like you." Eileen bent to pick a stalk of cow parsley. They were a quarter mile into their walk back to the estate. The evening was settling gently around them, its purple clouds sprawling overhead. "I know you said it wasn't my fight," she added quickly. "But...you know. Granny's come to live here. I have an interest in making sure she's in a stable place."

Ewan kicked a rock out of his way. "Jenkins is a parasite. He showed up a few months after my mother's death after the lord's personal assistant retired. He seemed fine at first—nice clothes, superb manners, but it was all a show. Turned out he'd been defrauding retirees for years in England."

"Wow. What does he scam? I mean, it's a nice castle and all, but isn't it kind of empty?"

Ewan nodded. "There's not a lot of jewels in the safe, if that's what you mean. But the man's earned the lord's esteem," he went on in imitation Queen's English.

"Meaning?"

"Meaning they trust him. They gradually let him take charge of things. He's signatory now on staff payroll and even deals with their investments. *She* even trusts him." Ewan threw a stick into the shrubs. "He got the lord to name him next of kin, if you can believe it, in case of emergency. And he thinks that makes him the Rutherford heir."

Eileen brought her hand to her mouth. No wonder Ewan hated him. He'd stolen Ewan's very birthright. She *knew* he wasn't satisfied being a shepherd the rest of his life, dragging his brother out of bars. And he looked so much older when he talked about Jenkins like this. Weary. Like he'd thrown his life out with the uneaten chips.

He was walking a good three paces too fast for Eileen now. As she jogged to keep up, she struggled for something to say. She'd been silent too long. But what consolation was there? If Emily was here, she'd know the right thing to say.

And then she found it. Ahead, inspiration. A few yards in front of them on the footpath was an enormous rectangular stone.

"Hey, what's that doing?" She approached the rock. It was gigantic, about four and a half feet tall, made of a gray-yellow mineral—sandstone maybe—covered on its shaded side with rosettes of lichen. Carved onto its surface was a spiral, sort of like a crop circle. It reminded Eileen of the Rutherford family headstones. "Is it a chimney?"

Ewan approached and removed a strand of ivy from the rock. "It's a megalith."

"What does that mean?"

"Giant stone. They're all over Britain. You probably know Stonehenge."

"Oh, right. This was made by the same people?"

"Not likely. Stonehenge is six thousand years old. This one is probably ninth century. It marks a battle victory."

"Who won?"

"No idea. Nick the Norse? I hear bits about the tribes from Granny, and Mr. Temple could talk your ear off. But there are so many stones it's hard to keep track. I always liked this fella." He stroked the top of the stone. "Looks just like a bloke. Some geezer waiting on his bus. You hear about drunks wandering about at night who run right into it. Knocks the daylights out of them. Folks in town call it the Sobering Stone."

Ewan looked at his watch and motioned for them to keep going.

She was doing better, Eileen considered. Ewan wasn't hurling sticks into the bushes anymore. She'd like to take his hand. Maybe first she'd dig a little deeper. "Why does Lady Rutherford wear the opera gloves?"

Ewan laughed feebly. "She's a funny old bird. I used to think she wanted to outdress everyone, but I don't actually think she cares about that kind of thing. It's either leftover mourning for my mother or a mark of respect to the miners who died. You know, black cloth, like an armband? She still feels responsible. It was her mine that exploded."

"How long ago was that?"

"A while. Twenty years ago, twenty-one."

"And your father was a miner?" She realized she was pushing it here. But it paid off.

Ewan took her hand as they approached the next intersection. He also moved Eileen gently to the right side of the sidewalk, nearest the hedgerow, keeping himself on the side with traffic.

"Dad spent ten years in the mine. And you know, he hated the dark." Ewan shook his head. "He swore it was cursed, too. He lost several friends to cave-ins. Said it was crazy to work underground. His first trade was animals, and he was the son of a farmer. But union wages paid double what you made in the fields. On weekends, though, he was always back with the sheep. He taught me and my brothers everything we know about them. I always wondered, after he left for the oil rig, how offshore work would satisfy him, no live heartbeats, nothing green. But then he only worked the rig two years. Fell off one night while I was away at school.

It was growing dark. They'd stayed at the games longer than Eileen had realized, and the light was fading. Most of the traffic from the festival had passed already, heading to Kirkcaldy, Leven, or Aberdeen. She was on an unfamiliar stretch of road.

"Is it much farther?" She asked. She was growing tired.

"Another twenty minutes. Do you want to rest?"

The roar of a car engine interrupted. It was approaching from the far side of a blind curve. Ewan nudged Eileen closer to the hedgerow.

"Stay well back."

The car neared but remained hidden by overgrowth.

"I'll wave to slow him down." Ewan gave her hand a squeeze. But surprisingly, he looked nervous.

"Ewan, don't." Eileen was scared, but she forced a smile. "Be careful."

He nodded, then put one foot onto the road.

The car was upon them. It was the Rutherfords' Bentley. With its tinted glass, it was impossible to see who was driving. But it was totally out of control. Ewan pumped his palm up and down motioning the driver to slow down.

But the driver sped *up*, making straight for them.

"Eileen, jump out of the way!" Ewan yelled.

"Where?" Eileen looked wildly for a safe place.

"There!" Ewan pointed to a tiny gap in the hedge. It was a corridor no wider than a mailbox. She squeezed herself in and pulled Ewan after her just before the car drove over the very spot of sidewalk where they'd been standing. It careened back onto the road and roared out of sight, leaving two tread marks smoking on the pavement. A pair of crows tore out of the hedgerow next to Eileen and shrieked at the disappearing taillights.

Ewan struggled out of the hedgerow and helped Eileen out after him.

"Who the hell was that?" Eileen gasped. "We were almost a hit-and-run!"

"Drunk," Ewan said, shading his eyes at the disappearing Bentley.

"Could it be Clyde? The Rutherfords' driver?"

Ewan shook his head. "He'd never risk his job. Someone else must have got behind the wheel."

"Maybe someone stole it!" Eileen's mind was racing, now, churning with the significance of a run-in with the town car. With the speed it was going and the driver's refusal to detour around them, that dude was *aiming* at them. She and Ewan were the only ones around. They were probably being followed! By someone from the games? Jenkins. Or Hugh! Both had reason to be mad at Ewan. He'd gotten in a fistfight with one and there was just plain bad blood with the other. Jenkins had access to the car keys and Hugh might know how to hotwire.

"Ewan?" she began. They were walking briskly now, and Ewan was muttering to himself. It was time to talk this out.

"Yeah?"

"Shouldn't we call the police?"

He raised an eyebrow. "What for? These are narrow roads with poor lighting. Some folks are just bad drivers."

"Um...I'm pretty sure that driver tried to hit us. And unless I was hallucinating, you and I both just crawled out of a sticker bush to avoid getting pulverized. Aren't you just a little bit concerned?"

Looking carefully in both directions, Ewan led Eileen across the street, past the Rutherford Castle Estate sign, and onto the pebble driveway that led to the farmhouse. "Scots drink," he said. "There isn't much else to do on long nights when you're surrounded by a hundred thousand sheep and don't get satellite TV."

She considered this. She was the newcomer. Was she merely observing rural driving trends? Or did she have a duty to point out a public menace? "There are people who'd probably like to get to you, Ewan," she said slowly. "People who'd like you out of the way? The lord and lady are capable of changing their will. Naming you, rightly, as castle heir. Remember all those Rutherfords in the tent?"

Ewan just shook his head and smiled.

"OK then. How 'bout Hugh? Even if he can't claim any inheritance, he's got a real chip on his shoulder. You were shouting at him at the pub, you disagree publicly all the time, and he's got an...addiction problem. And of course there's Jenkins." The list of crazy driver suspects was growing. It seemed endless. Hell, the Wharf waitress was probably after them. There was that beer glass she'd overturned.

But Ewan wasn't listening. He reached out instead and held her by the waist. "No one," he said firmly, "is out to get me." He rubbed her arms slowly. "Eileen," he breathed, "relax."

She opened her mouth to argue—about the wild driver, the tent full of daggers. And then he kissed her. He drew his fingers up her back. He kissed her eyes, her chin, her hair, her throat, her collarbone.

"Och, the snoggin' in these parts!" Mr. Temple's laughter rang out. "Need a lift?" He rolled down the passenger-side window of his red Mini.

Eileen pulled away first. She'd never been caught kissing in her life. Someone give me a paper bag to climb in!

Mr. Temple couldn't have cared less. "Hugh's passed out, Ewan. I left him on his bedroom floor. Couldn't lift him farther."

"Thanks, mate. Can you take the lass home? She got a scare on the road."

Eileen hesitated. Temple's face was sweaty and his eyes a little over-rubbed. The car radio was loud, and there were piles of dirty burlap on the backseat.

"You don't want a ride?" Ewan asked her.

"Last chance." Temple rolled up his window.

"I'll walk from here. Thanks anyway." She gave Ewan's arm a squeeze and then took off for the hill to the Red House.

Seventeen

Someone was pounding on the stairs. Or jumping on loose floorboards. Eileen raised herself on an elbow and noticed though her window that there were lights on in the castle. She'd never seen lights on over there this late. She shouldered her way into a robe and into the hallway.

Granny was hurrying from room to room in her nightgown.

"Granny, what is it?" She had misbuttoned her robe and put her sunglasses on by mistake. She pointed to the living room sofa, where a male figure lay. Eileen approached, figuring it was perhaps Clyde, asleep after too much ale. But it wasn't. It was Mr. Temple. At the foot of the couch her mother hovered.

Eileen gasped. His left cheek was scraped and bleeding. One eye was swollen shut. His clothes were muddied. His hair, normally tucked under a cap, stuck out like a scrubbing brush, and his arm hung at a weird angle in his overcoat.

"He had an accident," Joyce said.

Eileen pictured Mr. Temple sprawled on the road, the Bentley speeding into the distance.

"There's no emergency room for eighty miles." Fran wrung her hands. "So we've called the local doctor. Ewan left to pick him up ten minutes ago."

"How did it happen?" Eileen whispered.

"Someone let the bull out of his field, and he charged," Granny answered.

"Shouldn't we call an ambulance, Mom? Look at him? Did you check his vitals?"

"We checked," said Joyce. "Well, Ewan did. He's the one who dragged him here from the barley field."

"We really can't wait for a village doctor." Eileen reached for the phone. "Is emergency 911 here?" As she began to dial, Rowena appeared from the bathroom door and took the receiver from Eileen.

"Eileen, we can't call emergency services."

"Why not? Look at him. He's concussed and could have internal bleeding."

"We need a doctor who doesn't ask questions. The family's bull has charged an estate resident. Caedmon is the Rutherfords' bread and butter. See where I'm going?"

"No?"

"The constable told the Rutherfords that a single incident more with him, he'd get a bullet in the head. But how would the estate carry on without him? They don't make a living off the sheep."

Eileen fretted with the cord of her bathrobe.

"What I want to know"—Joyce bent over Mr. Temple and straightened his rumpled sleeve—"is who allowed that animal out. Poor man. He certainly has a broken arm, but think what else could have happened. Thank God Ewan showed up when he did."

Granny shook her head. "I wonder if it's safe to stay." She walked to the widow and stared at the castle. "I don't want to run into Caedmon when I go fill the bird feeder."

Joyce went to her mother and laid her hand on her shoulder. "The doctor should be here soon. Later we'll have to have a talk with the bull's keeper about precautions."

"That would be Hugh," Eileen murmured. Had Hugh done some night stalking of his own? Woken out of his stupor and sicced the bull on someone? With head trauma like he'd had, maybe he got morbidly wound up over small things, like show disqualifications. And maybe he *had* overdosed Caedmon and set him on Mr. Temple, who, well, might want Hugh's job. Could be the two of them were on worse terms than he and Ewan even. "Rowena. How long has Hugh been Caedmon's keeper?"

"Almost ten years. He's the most experienced handler with big animals the estate has had. After his father."

"Do the Rutherfords trust him?" Joyce asked.

"They must. They're the strictest people I ever met. Look how cautious they were about your visit. They won't be any different when it comes to their animals, especially one as significant as Caedmon."

There was suddenly a commotion downstairs. Charlie was baying and prancing in the entryway. The front door swung wide and through it came a disheveled man Eileen had never seen.

"Lounge is on the landing, Dr. Marshall," Ewan called after him. Marshall went straight for the couch, knelt beside his patient, and gave a brisk nod to Joyce, who moved out of the way.

Rowena and Eileen hovered nearby. Ewan took Charlie's collar and made some fast introductions.

Dr. Marshall lifted Mr. Temple's lids and shone a small flashlight into them. "Concussion," he said, and removed a small vial from his bag. The smell of camphor filled the room as he opened it. Briefly, he held the bottle under his patient's nose. He woke up with a start. "Steady," Dr. Marshall instructed. "Try not to move."

"My arm!"

"I'm going to relocate it."

Dr. Marshall rolled up the shirtsleeve of Mr. Temple's healthy arm and injected something into it. "That'll help," he told Temple. "Lad." He snapped his fingers. "Hold his good arm." Ewan did so. Dr. Marshall then bent Mr. Temple's injured arm across his chest and turned it to a ninety-degree angle. Mr. Temple howled.

Eileen clutched her mother's hand.

"Ready?" the doctor asked.

Mr. Temple took a deep breath and nodded.

Dr. Marshall straightened Temple's elbow and rotated the injured arm outward. Then he put his palm around Temple's wrist and pushed the shoulder joint back into the socket. The poor man moaned and pit rolled down his lip, but three seconds later there was a pop.

"There." He exhaled vigorously. "Back in joint." Marshall pushed a bottle of pills on Ewan. "Two every four hours for pain. No refills." Then he headed for the stairs. "And, lad, see that there's better care with that bull. This is my last stampede call. They'll have my license if another goes unreported."

There being nothing else to do for the injury victim, the household went to bed, Joyce sharing Eileen's bed so that Temple could recover in the privacy of her room. But as she lay awake in the hours before dawn, Eileen couldn't get the picture of Hugh out of her mind. Hugh with Caedmon on a leash, careening with a mug of beer, storming out of competition, pumping the feed trough with steroids. But would the man set a raging animal on his friend?

Eighteen

Eileen sat up in bed. Her mother was still asleep next to her. The night was still. No moon or starlight shone through the curtains. The windowpane had been lifted, though, and there again was the rope. Like the time before, the rope led to the window and over the side of the house. Eileen slipped out of bed as quietly as she could.

She felt no danger as she approached the open window, which was strange. She'd been trembling with fear at Emily's appearance in the yard. This time, it was like she'd been hypnotized or slipped a mild tranquilizer. Some internal instinct urged her to the rope and then coaxed her downward. From the pastureland, she heard the bagpipes. Joyce turned over, humming the bagpipes melody, then fell back asleep. Eileen returned to the window, took a deep breath, grabbed the rope, and gradually lowered herself down it. It was soundless, her descent, like sliding down a banister. She didn't even chafe in her hands.

Hugh was waiting for her at ground level. He wore a highwayman's coat with a tall stiff collar and a stovepipe hat. He looked like Jack the Ripper. He took her hand and led her into the fields. They began to climb the hill. The barley stalks scratched Eileen's legs and mud sucked at her feet. Hugh urged her on. With just her thin pajamas, she was quickly soaked. There was no stopping Hugh, though, and together they climbed to the crest of the hill.

"Ewan?" she called, expecting to see him with his pipes. She was at the very spot where they had met.

But Ewan wasn't there. In his place was Caedmon. The bull flashed into view from behind a copse of trees and stood there panting. If he hadn't been so enormous and so alarming, Eileen would have reached a hand out to touch him, to see if he might break apart into dust and shadow.

He was far too fierce to touch, though. His eyes were bloodshot, and his coat was thick with grime. Bright red wounds showed on his hide. He had been tortured! And yet despite this cruel treatment, the bull was still a fortress. Like the castle that had born him. His wooly shoulders hulked above his triangle head and steam rose from his nostrils.

Then he ran.

Hugh disappeared into the trees. The bull was bearing down, head lowered.

"Call him off!" Eileen wailed.

But Hugh stood silent, silk hat low on his forehead, arms crossed over his chest. He finally removed a walking stick from the folds of his cape and held it out, parallel with the ground. He swirled it in a circle and pointed it at Eileen.

Caedmon roared. Nearer and nearer he came, like a rocket from the grave.

In a flash, a figure ran in front of Eileen—a female in a white T-shirt. Emily? Only now she was much more solid. No more wispy shadows. Eileen could see her completely now, from her tangled red hair and purple Doc Martins to the pewter varnish on her nails. She was radiant and strong. She stopped midway between Eileen and the oncoming bull and held up her hand.

"No!" Eileen shouted. "You'll be crushed!"

"But I won't," Emily said, her voice sort of in stereo, echoing from four directions at one time. "The bull can't hurt me."

But with that it was upon her. Clouds gathered around the three of them, and in the distance, the bagpipe tune resumed.

"Restore what's his," Emily's voice resonated. "Find the boy and restore what's his."

"But they don't listen to me!" Eileen shouted. Tears welled in her eyes. She braced for impact, sure the bull would skewer her straight through. But Caedmon ran right *through* the ghost and then through Eileen, too, a macabre hologram. A shock wave ripped the scene in two, and Eileen woke up on the floor next to her bed.

"Goodness! You fell," Joyce said. "You all right, Eileen?"

"Uhh." She struggled to her feet and made her way to the bedroom door. Then she went out to the hallway and to the living room, which had the best view of the surrounding fields. It was dawn but barely. Enough light to see by. She put her face up to the glass. There was no sign of a struggle in the yard or nearby fields. No animal prints in the wet earth. But she heard the bagpipe, for real, this time, sad and low and howling in the distance.

Nineteen

The next day, Clyde and Jenkins moved Temple to the castle. The Rutherfords thought it best to keep him there rather than moving him back to his cottage in Leven. Less speculation, fewer questions. Jenkins brought Lord Rutherford's own wheelchair for Mr. Temple, and he was given one of the lord's best guest rooms.

A day later, the castle cook, Daphne, sent word that they could pay a visit. Granny, who had made good friends with Daphne over soup recipes, was anxious to see how Mr. Temple was doing. She packed him a couple pies, a pint of gooseberries, a new loaf of bread, and a single bottle of beer (which had been in the back of the fridge "for God knows how long," but which Rowena thought Mr. Temple would appreciate.)

Granny knocked at the door of the servants' entrance, which everyone except the Rutherfords used.

"Good morning, liedies!" The woman Eileen assumed must be Daphne threw wide the door. "Temple will be glad to see you. What a scare he gave us. Thank God Ewan found him. But mum's the word, a' course. His room ain't far."

Now *inside* the castle, after weeks of skittering through the underbrush to avoid being seen through its windows, Eileen was a little underwhelmed. For five long minutes, Daphne let them along darkpaneled corridors. It seemed like miles of hallway, only every few yards by a padlocked door. Where were the marble sculptures and rare paintings? Eileen had seen car-sized chandeliers and corridors of glass in postcards of the French castles. These bare hallways were more like an empty garage than a centuries' old estate. And shouldn't there be a maid or footman balancing a tea tray?

"How much farther?" Eileen looked at her watch.

"I know what you're thinking, miss," Daphne said.

"You do?"

"Where's the fine tapestries? The gilt picture frames?"

"Sort of…"

"And why ain't there more finery?" Daphne added with an eyebrow. Eileen nodded.

"You h'ain't been behind the scenes at a stately home before. And this one was grand once. Had a stable full of hunters and a fleet of town cars. These hallways had embroidered settees and family portraits. There was even a court musician on loan to us once. But since the mine disaster, well, the lord and lady closed up most 'a the rooms. Don't want to spend the money heatin' 'em. They keep furniture in the three rooms they use plus my suite on the top floor and one guest room. Times is hard in Scotland, lass. Even for the titled folks."

As she finished, Daphne led them through the final yards of corridor and into an atrium. It, too, was paneled in chestnut, but unlike the low-pitched hallways of the last five minutes, this ceiling vaulted upward like a cathedral. Set into the high walls were stained-glass windows, and at the apex of the ceiling was an enormous wooden chandelier made of deer horns. Fifteen racks, at least. Animal-head trophies dotted the walls, and in the center of the room stood a magnificent marble table. A spiral staircase stretched up three floors from the ground and led to a balcony that overlooked the atrium. Lady Rutherford was leaning on the balustrade, waiting for them.

"Rowena." She smiled. "I see you've brought a crowd. You'd better come up."

She beckoned them to climb the stairs to the third level. "Mr. Temple will be glad for visitors. He's only had us and Jenkins."

They climbed the staircase and followed Lady Rutherford down another long corridor to a guest room. It was much more cheerful than the corridors. Not Buckingham Palace but an improvement on the antlers and ironwork. A hand-stitched floral carpet covered the floor. The curtains in rich green velvet hung from valances above two picture windows. The bed where Mr. Temple lay with a book on his chest was a dark polished wood with a carved balcony overhead. Next to it was a pair of matching side tables, each with deer-foot legs and Tiffany-style lamps.

The room had a few dents in its armor. The curtains, though expensive-looking, were patched in several places. Eileen could see the darning of a skilled seamstress on several sections. The carpet, too, was threadbare near the door, and another area about two feet wide had eroded where it met the bed. The lampshade on the closer of the two night tables was chipped in a couple places.

Eileen had nothing like these ornaments at her own house, but if she had, she'd certainly go out of her way to keep them in good shape. She wondered if the Rutherfords' age meant they didn't see imperfections so well anymore. Maybe they'd stopped caring. Or else the person they paid to take care of things didn't really do so.

As they approached Mr. Temple's bedside, Lady Rutherford motioned to the nearby chairs. "Dr. Marshall thought we'd better not move him, so we've asked if his family will let us keep him until he's more comfortable."

"Will it be a long recovery?" Joyce asked.

"It depends on how quickly his arm heals. And after a concussion, at his age, you never know. We're very lucky it wasn't...well, we're very lucky."

He was in a half doze under a fluffy white comforter. He wore scarlet pajamas a good size too small. As Eileen cast around the room, Jenkins walked in from a door set in the paneling. He had a pair of man's pants draped over one arm and a cell phone. "Yes, twenty-five milligrams. Clyde will pick it up this afternoon." He clicked shut his phone and stowed it in the pocket of his blazer. Today's tie read *Elizabeth Regina: 50* in vertical script down the front.

"So, you're nursemaid, too, along with everything else?" Rowena flicked a hair out of her eyes.

"Well. Why not? We're colleagues and friends. Don't want any harm to come to the old man."

Rowena cleared her throat loudly. "I'll bet."

A noise came from Temple at that. "Not to fear," he mumbled. "Temple's still here!" He leaned forward a couple inches from his over-stuffed pillows.

"Temple!" they chorused.

Jenkins leaped to adjust his pillow.

"I'm all right!" Temple said, rather loudly. Jenkins glared at him, rather severely, Eileen thought.

"At the castle you're under our care," the butler said, smoothing Temple's comforter so it pulled tighter over his chest. "You'll give us leave to tend to you, will you not?"

It seemed like a loaded question.

Mr. Temple gave a tiny nod and Jenkins backed away. But Temple kept his eyes trained on the other man for the next several minutes as he flitted about checking this and readjusting that.

"How are you feeling?" Eileen asked, following Temple's gaze and studying Jenkins as he draped the pants he'd been carrying on a wooden clothes stand, pulled out a drawer, removed a prescription bottle, frowned at its label, and put it away. Then he examined a set of papers on a brass tray and wrote something with a fountain pen in the margin. His signature?

Temple cleared his throat. "I'm much better. Thanks, Eileen, Ms. Morgan, ladies. Got a good knockin' is all. Nothin' to get alarmed about."

"Was it horrible?" Eileen asked. "Were you nearly gored?"

Joyce nudged her.

"What?"

"Aye, lass." Temple nodded. "It was horrible. Good thing Caedmon dropped me in a wee puddle and didn't fling me off the cliff." He chuckled wearily.

Rowena pitched her chair back so it pivoted on its cat's paw feet. "So, Andrew. How'd it happen?"

"I was walking back home from the farm 'round eleven. I'd left me Mini there for Dan, who wanted to borrow it the next day, Hugh being in need of the truck." As he spoke, Temple checked now and then on Jenkins, who hovered. Poking linens, correcting hems.

"It was dark." Temple continued, "I missed my turn. Before I knew it, I was down on me face in the dirt, fifteen hundred pounds of bull breathing on me. Bloody stupid, I 'spect. Beggin' your pardon." He looked at Lady Rutherford and the other women. "I should have organized a lift. But there we are. I was walking down the wrong path, and I felt something come up behind me, big as a barn it seemed, only roaring and pounding. Next thing I know, I'm in the Red House having me arm pulled out of its socket." He laughed despite the look on Joyce's and Fran's face. "Och, it's not so bad. I've dislocated my shoulder before. You'll see how fast it mends. You might just want to take care on the property, though." He rubbed at the bandage on his forehead. "Especially at night. That Caedmon's as cunning as Lucifer."

Fran fussed with her handbag a moment. "Rowena, did you know about this before renting us the Red House? I had no idea Caedmon was still stampeding people."

"It seemed...contained." Rowena shrugged.

Lady Rutherford nodded. "That's what the vet assured us. Very rare behavior. Wouldn't happen again with the correct diet and sedative combination."

But Joyce didn't look convinced. She took her mother's hand. "Maybe newcomers upset the bull. Could we have brought something out in him? Via scent or, I don't know, foreign endorphins?"

All this time, Jenkins had continued tidying around them. He cleared up a tray of breakfast dishes; he went through several letters. He pulled a bell cord near the door, and Clyde showed up, took a piece of paper from him, and disappeared. In between tasks, Jenkins shot Eileen glances. At first deadpan but gradually more fierce.

Yeah, I'm onto you, she brain-waved him. *I know you're cooking the castle books. You and Hugh. Or you and some townie follower. Probably mixed poison into Hugh's beer while you were at it and poured a measure into Caedmon's feed.*

Despite his cowering at the games that time, here in the castle Jenkins was poised and comfortable. He came across sort of servile, but he also had access to stuff you'd never expect: prescriptions, documents, calling for servants.

"I understand your anxiety, Joyce," Lady Rutherford said, "but I'm sure Caedmon's behavior had nothing to do with you or Eileen or Fran. There's got to be a reason for it, and I plan to speak to Hugh about it this very afternoon. Though he's been reckless in the past, he is, on the whole, a good employee. Thanks to him, we are owners of the most famous animal in Fife. He'll account for this, though." She nodded at Temple.

She turned to Jenkins next, who was straightening Mr. Temple's blankets one more time. "That'll be all, Earnest. If you don't mind."

He knit his brows together and opened his mouth to say something. There was an intense look between himself and Lady Rutherford, but then he seemed to reconsider, bowed slightly, picked up a breakfast tray, and left.

Temple seemed to have fallen asleep, and Eileen was glad to see that he had a very contented look on his face.

"What exactly does that man do here?" Eileen asked Lady Rutherford once Jenkins was a safe distance away.

"Earnest? He's advisor to the laird. And he keeps the books, and the schedule, and..." She sighed. "He and the laird have become close friends. Before his stroke, they used to go hunting."

Eileen considered this. *Would outdoor sports endear a manservant so well he became signatory on important documents? He was a commoner? A Pom commoner.* "Does he do any driving for the laird?"

"Eileen!" her mother whispered.

"It's all right, Joyce." Lady Rutherford gestured her consent. "Young lady, we hired Jenkins to do for an elderly couple the tasks they can no longer do for themselves. And, as you have heard, Jenkins and the laird are friends." She smoothed her floral skirt across her knees. It had come unstitched along the bottom hem. Did she know? Why had no one pointed that out to her, her, a great lady and all? She reached into the pocket of her cardigan and withdrew her black gloves.

"Jenkins is also a great friend of Mr. Temple's here. Both men have been loyal. Both keep quiet." At that, she gave Eileen a penetrating stare. It made Eileen want to look the other way, but she clenched her jaw and kept still. "And if you must know, your informers are correct. He is next of kin to the lord. May even wind up being heir. Not that I agreed to it. But the laird put it in writing last year. So it's official. Jenkins could be the next Lord Rutherford."

There was quiet in the room. Fran stared at the floor. Eileen blinked hard. Joyce licked her lips. Rowena sipped tea.

Lady Rutherford got up and moved about the room. "To fully answer your question, though. What Jenkins does for us? He serves the laird as an assistant and a driver, as does Mr. Temple when Clyde has a day off. Jenkins has taken over the duties our children didn't want. He helps with our travel, our documents, our shopping and medications, and our legal affairs. He gets a simple wage and our constant gratitude. So one day"—she approached the wide picture window—"we'll repay him."

Eileen screwed up the courage to say the thing that for so long needed saying. "And Ewan?"

A stillness hit the room. No one seemed to breathe. Lady Rutherford didn't move from the window. Rowena finally rose from her chair and fussed with Temple's blankets. Eileen wasn't backing down, though. Not today. Cocktail conversation was over. *Restore what's his*, the ghost had told her. Even if Ewan had let go all hope of reuniting with the Rutherfords, his mother couldn't rest. So important was this task it had made Emily entrust her mission to a total stranger. No matter what Ewan said to the contrary, your name mattered, your connection to others, your place in this world. And it mattered enough here that people were getting hurt.

"Ewan will get his education," Lady Rutherford finally said. She wouldn't face Eileen, though. Her body leaned heavily against the window frame, her eyes focused on some distance. "And he will always have a home on the farm. But the laird has made it clear." Her voice caught on that last word, *clear*. "Ewan is not a Rutherford."

With that, the lady walked toward the door, opened it, and disappeared into the paneled corridor.

Twenty

"What did you say that for?"

They had been ushered quickly from the castle by a very tight-lipped Daphne. And the door had been practically slammed after them.

"Family affairs are none of your business!" Joyce rubbed her temples as they speed-walked back to the Red House.

Eileen was not about to apologize, though. Not for embarrassing her mother or getting the boot out of the castle. She was proud she'd finally spoken up. "Don't you think their grandchild should be entitled to something?"

Rowena caught up to Eileen and, to her surprise, took her hand. "I know what you're trying to do. But it's not really your affair. Ewan's not ambitious, and he's not likely to cross his grandparents. Look how mad the old man is. He thinks children are dangerous, for goodness' sake. But Ewan." She clicked her teeth. "That boy cares too much about this place to trouble the waters. It would ruffle the feathers of that fool lord, might influence him to start throwing people off his land, people who've worked for him all their lives. Ewan's not willing to get stuck in that position. He loves the farm and his brothers too much."

"He's entitled to a castle, Rowena! And as for loving his brothers... what about their drinking? Remember Hugh at the Wharf? It was even worse at the games the other night. Hugh got plastered when Caedmon was thrown out of a competition. And Danny's friends were so wasted Ewan and I had to walk so we didn't have to share a ride home with them."

"Well, it may be time you had more supervision." Joyce yanked the door open, and the Red House portico shook briefly. "You've been telling me you're just out walking the dog."

"Don't worry, Joyce," Rowena followed on her heels. "There's not much trouble in Fife." She gave Eileen a wink. "With all the codgers out chasing errant cows, Eileen practically has a nanny."

Thanks, Rowena, Eileen brain-waved. Odd, though, Rowena sticking up for her like that.

Joyce put both hands on her hips. "Well, don't mess with the Rutherfords anymore, Eileen. I'm serious. Rowena and my mother are just tenants. If the castle thinks we're meddlers, Granny could lose her place at the Red House."

All four of them slunk into the house and retreated to their rooms.

Three days passed. Eileen played solitaire, checkers, crosswords. Where was Ewan? Couldn't he at least text her? She was way overdue telling him about being commissioned to get his fortune back. And what good was she to anyone cooped up with paranoid old ladies? And since her sick-room outburst, Eileen wasn't going to get any support from her mother or grandmother on her fortune-hunting plans. Cowards. They knew Ewan was being cut off. And that old lord was such a complacent old goat, sitting in his sedan chair while everyone tripped and groveled.

Three days came and went. No word from the castle. Nothing from Ewan or the farm. Then, on the fourth day—miraculously—the doorbell rang. Ewan, finally? Rowena answered the door and what followed was monotone conversation followed by: "Eileen, visitor!"

It was not Ewan in the entrance hall but a strange old woman. One who looked 115. Her chin was all gizzard, she had a toddler-sized hump on her back, and over it she wore a knit cardigan inside out. A dense thatch of white hair perched on her head, but her eyes were alert and searching. She reminded Eileen of an elaborate puppet. Like everyone, she wore rubber boots, though hers were bright orange.

"You, girl." Her searching eyes located Eileen above the foyer.

"Yes?" *Does she know me?*

"Andrew wants you fir tea. Hurry up. Taxi's downstairs."

Joyce poked her head around a corner. "She's grounded from paying visits, unless I come, too."

"If you have to," the old lady said.

"Who's Andrew?" Eileen asked.

"Och, for the love of God, Andrew Temple, girl. Who else? You comin' or what?"

"OK. Mom, I guess if Mr. Temple and Mrs...." She petered out.

"Eunice Temple, his grandmother."

"Right...so, OK. But..." Eileen threw a *help me* glance at her mother. "But we can't be late for your music lesson at two."

"What on earth are you talking about, Eileen? I'll just get my things."

"Good, and bring tea and biscuits while you're about it," the old lady told Joyce.

With that, the old woman went back the way she came. A "Rowena" over her shoulder by way of good-bye.

"Good to see you, Mrs. Temple." Rowena gestured for Eileen to follow.

Eileen grabbed her jacket and the packet of tea bags her mother thrust at her and ducked out the door after Mrs. Temple. Joyce followed, and, awkwardly, the three women bundled into the back of an awaiting taxi driven by, of all people, Bruce the Ruth.

"Afternoon," he said without looking up from the steering wheel.

If Mr. Temple is, say, sixty-five, Eileen reasoned as they pulled away, that would make his grandmother at least 105. Was that possible? Maybe she had that fish oil and flax seed diet. Eileen had ever seen so much extra skin or a hump. It was like Santa's sack.

Ten awkward minutes later, the old lady leaped to attention. "Here's the place!"

"Yes, Mrs. Temple." Bruce the Ruth smiled. "I know it, ma'am."

The row house was one of six two-story structures on the outskirts of Leven. It was one of the very homes they had ridden past on their way from the train station, the apartments with the idle children. There was no one loitering today, though. The street was empty. The Temples lived at number 1559 behind a once green door (now gray) with a horseshoe knocker. The knocker had been knocked so hard, it hung in a C instead of a U.

Mrs. Temple pulled herself up the handrail to the door, unlocked it, and swung it open so hard it almost slapped Eileen on its backswing. She caught it with her shoulder and let her mother in behind her. A ghoulish bowling alley looked back at Eileen. She took the tea bags out of her pocket. "Uh, where do you keep the tea?"

"Kettle's in the kitchen." Mrs. Temple made her way past a broken coat tree, a grandfather clock, and empty birdcage. She threw her cardigan across the back of an overstuffed chair in the next room and began poking at an ivy on her mantle piece. When she observed Eileen hesitating, she straightened.

"Andrew!" she shouted at the ceiling. "Get down here and help this American make a pot of tea!"

"Actually, I've made tea at the Red House all summer."

"Bully for you."

A bleary-eyed Andrew Temple came struggling down the staircase. "Yes, Gran, all right." He took the tea bags from Eileen with an apologetic smile.

If Mr. Temple had invited anyone to tea, he'd done it in a sleep delirium. Look at him! Why couldn't his grannie let him sleep? And why on earth did she want guests anyway? Look at this place.

"Och, teenagers, out of the kitchen," Mrs. Temple said, pushing Eileen toward a lumpy couch in the living room. "Joyce? Step lively. You help Andrew. Can't have a Yank meddling with tea. Come sit here, Eileen." The old lady threw some pillows aside to make room on the couch for two. "Word in the village is you like to stir things up. I hear you started a pub brawl and broke a whole set of the Rutherfords' china."

Eileen was about to protest, but the old lady's eyes fell in an instant. Like that, she was asleep. A feather from her wing chair sat tethered on her chin. It rose and fell daintily with the lady's breathing.

"Asleep?" Mr. Temple called from the kitchen.

"Just dropped off." She felt like Red Riding Hood. Was there a smaller Granny in there, somewhere?

Joyce brought a tray of tea, cups, scones, and cookies into the living room. Since the coffee table was covered with several days of newspapers, a visitor's guide to Franplona, Spain, and a pile of men's socks, Joyce propped the tray on her lap and served everyone from there.

"Can I use the bathroom?" Eileen asked.

Temple nodded. "Down the hall, second on the left. How much longer you visiting your mother, Mrs. Morgan?" he said to Joyce.

"Until about the fifth of August. Problem is she's gotten very nervous about the bull."

Eileen made her way to the bathroom. Like the living room, it had become a library of discarded books and magazines. Stacks of gardening catalogs leaned against the wall. *Lawns of Legend*, a veritable encyclopedia, lay underneath the soap dispenser. Another title, *Hounds and Herbs*, leaned against the bath. Several Post-its stuck out of its pages. *Bovine Anatomy* lay across the back of the toilet tank. As Eileen approached the sink to wash her hands, she noticed a smudge on the medicine cabinet mirror. As she wiped it with her elbow, the mirror door opened just a little.

Curiosity took charge. There wasn't much in the cabinet, though: a couple ancient perfume bottles, extra soap and toilet paper, three pharmacy containers. Thinking she'd check the painkiller Temple had been prescribed, to see if it was one she knew, Eileen removed one of the orange bottles.

Animal X: Growth Hormone, it read. That wasn't painkiller. That was a doping agent! Some of her classmates used growth hormone before track meets. But what would a gardener do with it?

Oh—fix livestock competitions! Hello, smoking gun. Now didn't most people know that steroids wrecked the body and made some people crazy paranoid? The RX label had *Caedmon, adult bull* written on it, loud and clear. So Temple had been messing with the Rutherfords' stud *and* ruining Hugh's reputation in the process, not to mention launching an inadvertent missile across the estate. So how did Temple get *himself* stampeded? Occupational hazard? Maybe he and Hugh were in cahoots to ruin the bull through back alley pharmaceuticals and then at some later point miraculously cure him?

Think, Eileen!

How would an actual investigator solve this? Take samples from a crime scene, record evidence. That was it—photo evidence. She shot two pictures of the steroid bottle's RX label with her phone, one close-up and another of the vanity table where it was sitting among the soap and toothbrush clutter. If this *was* the trigger agent, Temple or Hugh or both of them together were cheating in high-stakes competition and using the animal against folks who interfered. Wow, like Emily!

Eileen was shaking slightly. She was doing it, solving a mystery, with illicit drugs, weapon, exhibit A. She wondered if Emily had found this bottle and been ready to squeal even.

Now that Caedmon had been thrown out of competition, was Temple about to disappear? Eileen would have to keep him around, long enough to link the clues, anyway, so she could turn over sufficient evidence of—what?—manslaughter by bovine proxy.

With a slightly trembling hand, she returned the bottle to the cabinet and very gently closed the door. Then she made her way back toward the Temples' living room.

Passing through the corridor, though, Eileen's eye caught on a doorway she'd missed earlier. Peering through, the interior was covered, floor to ceiling, in cabinetry. Each shelf held a number of identical glass cases, curio cabinets. Inside each was a miniature animal—deer, dogs, mice, sheep, owls, cats, frogs, insects. There were human figures, too—angels, noblemen, musicians, acrobats, fairy-tale maidens and trolls. Eileen had never seen such a horde. She wondered if they were Mr. Temple's or his grandmother's. They might be worth something.

She would take a closer look. Like any eBay junkie knew, the collector keeps the tags on. It was the same with these. One cubby's ballet dancer figurine was leaning slightly outward, in danger of falling. Eileen reached out and pushed it gently back to center. Then she got a look at the label: *1925 Art Deco bronze, Joseph Descombs.*

That must be worth a month's wage. And you didn't collect all this on a lawn-care salary. Either the Temples were secretly loaded or they had another source of income. Eileen stretched her hand out again to touch the ballerina. It was bronze. It wouldn't break.

She picked up the little dancer, light as a baby bird, smooth, cool, lustrous. It was a child dancer performing a pirouette. One of her knees jutted out at ninety degrees so that the entire statue balanced on a single toe point. Around the little girl's neck was the starched collar of a circus clown. She smiled jauntily like she was turning for an admirer whose pocket she was about to pick.

Eileen turned it over in her hands. Her mother's best china had the artist's signature on the bottom. Eileen turned the dancer over, but rather than the swirly initials she expected to see, there was a cork insert. Instinctively, she pulled on it. From inside the figure's leg dropped a syringe, its cylinder still red from use.

"There's a copy of that at Christie's website, if you're interested."

Though she was kneeling on the floor with her treasure, Eileen lurched at the sound of Mr. Temple's voice. He was leaning casually against the doorjamb. Eileen rose to her feet but smacked her head against a nearby shelf and dropped her statue.

With Wolverine speed, Temple stretched his torso and caught the little girl mid fall. "Got it!" But the syringe dropped onto the floor.

Eileen gasped.

"Urh. Sorry to startle you." Mr. Temple placed his body midway between Eileen and the fallen syringe. "Had to answer the call of nature and thought you might like a tour of the collection."

"I'm sorry." Eileen rubbed her injured head. "I'm snooping. I've just never seen so many collectibles."

"I don't mind." He waved her off. Then he bent down, picked up the syringe, and placed it awkwardly along the top shelf next to a Scottie dog. "You didn't pocket anything, right?" He replaced the dancing girl in her cabinet and closed the glass door with a click. "It's amazing what a lifetime of collecting looks like." He massaged his shoulder. "Did you notice this one here?"

He's going to pretend I didn't see that syringe, Eileen realized. He's going to stuff it in a box and ignore it! She knew where she'd seen it before, in Caedmon's field. When it fell out of Hugh's pocket after the bull's social training the night of the Wharf trip.

Mr. Temple flicked a light switch. Ceiling mounted lights came on, and spot lit the curios from various points above. Mr. Temple unfolded a library-style stepladder that had been leaning against the wall, put on a pair of white gloves, and brought down what looked to Eileen like an axe blade. Upon closer inspection, though, she saw it was probably a chip off a larger stone. There were markings on its surface—a carved line from a sure, steady tool. The carving resembled an animal, something with hooves and a tail, anyway, which wound elaborately around its back legs. The animal was missing its front third, from the shoulders upward, but from the waist down it was clearly a bull.

"Can I touch it?"

Temple nodded and handed Eileen one of his archival gloves. She put it on and ran her finger over the carving, tracing the line of the bull's back. "How old do you think it is?"

"The style is pre-Roman." He stuck his chest out a little.

"Wow!"

"It's most likely a copy. Jenkins found it on the beach, thought I'd like it for my collection." He rubbed the carving fondly.

"Really?" She was surprised. Jenkins's giving away something valuable.

"So he doesn't collect, himself?" She thought of all those times Jenkins had been seen digging around the property.

"Him, Lord no. He's keen on coats of arms and expensive suits. You know what he pays for those dinner jackets?"

Eileen shook her head. He went on to tell a story about buying the man an Edinburgh tie.

Temple was still rubbing his bull carving. "Those Pom historians thought this stone wasn't important enough to take back to London. But it's special to me." He gently replaced it in its cubby and turned it a few times on its pedestal. "My collection is imitations. Nice ones but for the most part forgeries of older pieces."

"You know that, and you collect them anyway?"

"You know what a real Pictish carving of this clarity would cost?" He pointed back to the cabinet.

Why did he look angry?

"Course you don't. You'd have no idea what they would cost. I have a modest assembly here of near-originals. Many appear in catalogs. Windsor Castle's antiquarian once called for a tip on a Delft miniature, and I was glad to give him a photograph of my spaniel, there." He took down a ceramic dog and turned it in the light.

Eileen didn't know how to reply. "It's...cute."

"It's certainly not cute. It's...perfection." Temple cleared his throat. Was he crying?

"Sorry about that bang on yer head before. Let's see what's doing in the lounge." With that, he replaced the dog, turned off the museum lighting, and left the room. Eileen was alone then with a syringe staring at her from a top shelf.

What did she do? Smash it. No. Take it. Yes. No. He'd see it was missing. Replace it with a decoy. No—that wouldn't make any difference at all. Plus she didn't have a decoy. Think, think. She searched the room for ideas. Well, she could always take another picture with her phone. She wasn't sure what a photo of a used syringe was evidence of, but it seemed important to document it.

She got out her phone. There was just enough battery life for a couple more shots. She climbed up to the top of the curio cabinet on the library ladder, took three pictures of the syringe, one from the outside of the glass cabinet, to establish where it was, and two more close-up. For good measure, she took a picture of the bull rune, too.

Because she didn't dare save the photos on her phone, and because her mother was calling "Eileen, tea," she e-mailed the photos to Ewan and quickly hit the "delete" button on her photo album. She just had to hope there had been enough service in Leven to send the files properly.

Mr. Temple's grandmother had woken up while Eileen was out and was bossing Joyce around like the empress of Bombay. "Pay the florist!" A moment later: "Get that cat out of here; don't tell me to wash my neck. I'll do it when I'm good and ready!"

Eventually Joyce persuaded the old lady to take some tea, but she just thrust it back and stormed up the stairs.

"Dementia." Temple smiled apologetically.

Joyce put her hand on his shoulder. "How long? You poor man."

"Longer than you'd think." He looked thoroughly exhausted. Crooks tire easy, Eileen considered. Must be all the lying. "Shall I give ye girls a lift home?"

Eileen felt her phone buzz in her pocket. "Got a ride, thanks!" Eileen grinned at her phone's display. The long-awaited text had finally arrived.

Be there in 5, E.

Good as his word, in 5, there he was.

"Thanks for coming, Ewan." Joyce sat next to him in the front while Eileen bounced around the loosely sprung backseat. She twirled her hair around her finger. Of all the times for Mom to take the front seat! She had so much to tell Ewan! It had been ages since their last kiss. Didn't she realize that in this century, kids her age made out? What was the point in chaperones? Kids just necked on park benches if they had to.

"It's no problem, Mrs. Morgan. Danny said he saw you drive in with Bruce and I was on my way back from the shops." He lifted an eyebrow in the rearview and mouthed to Eileen, "Soon."

Twenty-One

Just as he dropped Joyce and Eileen back at the Red House, Ewan got a call from his brother. Danny had set fire to something in the farmhouse. He was trying his hand at cookery and, according to Ewan, had a few accidents "around the cooktop."

From the Red House doorstep, Eileen watched Ewan drive away. Again. Would he tell someone about the steroids or the syringe she'd found? Would he confront Hugh about why Mr. Temple had medical supplies for the Rutherfords' most valuable animal? Or why Jenkins was turning up "nearly real" Pictish objects? Would Ewan ever kiss her again?

She'd have to hold that fantasy for the moment, though. Lie low. Her confrontation with Lady Rutherford and her snooping at Mr. Temple's had probably invited more attention than she'd like. Even Mr. Temple's grandmother had called her a meddler.

There had to be somewhere she could go, though, to gather a little more information on this mystery. Think, think. Ah! The cave. That's where the English archaeologists thought the valuable artifacts would be. It was also where Ewan had first introduced Emily. Her ghost might come see her again there and explain what she was supposed to do at this point. She needed a guide in this drama. The cave was the place.

Eileen rifled through her suitcase and took out a white T-shirt like Emily's. It wasn't a concert tee, but it had a logo across the front—*Tweet This*. Ridiculous, but the right idea. She squeezed on her skinny jeans. Then, pulling on the rubber boots and anorak, she looked in the mirror. She was a little like Emily. Not a lot—but kind of. Loosening her hair from its ponytail, she slipped down the stairs, holstering Charlie's leash on the way.

"Where are you going?" Rowena called after her.

"Out." No point explaining. But then she reconsidered. She didn't want to get chaperoned at the cave, so she softened. "I'm collecting wildflowers. I'll bring some back for our table."

Joyce came out of her room, put her hands on her hips, and looked stern. "Don't forget dinner's at seven."

Eileen took the path past the castle toward the garden and the cave. It wasn't the best day for a walk. The fog had returned, and midges nibbled at her neck. "Charlie, come on!" He was headstrong today. What had gotten into him? One moment, he clung to her leg, the next he was straining at the leash. Finally, she'd had enough. "Go on then!" She unclipped his collar.

With a yelp, he bolted and scampered back over the cobblestones toward the Red House.

So much for loyalty. And what had spooked him? Maybe it was the fog. It looked like it was alive today, gathering and dispersing, clinging to trees, then crawling like dry ice vapor along the ground. Water particles danced in front of Eileen's eyes. From every direction, she could hear dripping from sodden leaves and wet farm equipment. It was nearly a whiteout.

The garden wall ought to be near. The place where she'd learned what a stile was. She held her arms out straight. There, contact. The wall. Cold, solid, reliable. Its chinking gouged here and there from storms. She felt her way across the stile and climbed over. Then she searched the underbrush for the clearing that indicated the cave path. Most of the area was choked with roots and bushes, but a few paces past the wall she saw the trampled path. Fog swirled, but Eileen could just make out the low-hanging bough she had hit her temple against.

A deep drone sounded somewhere offshore. Fog horn? The train on the Forth Bridge? If this kind of whiteout was common, there was no wonder Ewan's father fell off the rig.

The water particles merged together up ahead, but suddenly within the swirl there stood a woman. She had her back turned to Eileen and unmistakable auburn hair.

"Emily?"

"Goodness, no, girl! I'm no ghost. I'm Daphne. Castle cook."

"Oh. Hi." Eileen tried not to sound disappointed.

"What are you doing out in this mire?"

"I'm on my way to the bay."

"Och, then you might well meet the ghost." Daphne repositioned her shopping basket in the crook of her arm. "She likes the fog." As she said this, she reached into the basket, withdrew a sprig of parsley, and tossed it over her shoulder. "I know—silly. I'm a wee bit superstitious. But I've got good grounds, where I work. You ever hear the noises at night?"

Eileen nodded energetically. Finally, she thought. Someone with their guard down!

Daphne wiped her brow with a corner of her apron. "Care to come in for a bit a' tea?"

As they entered the castle, Daphne gestured for Eileen to take one of the pinewood chairs tucked under the butcher-block kitchen table. She went to the kitchen counter and poured water from an electric kettle into a teapot, then brought down two china cups from an overhead cabinet and offered one to Eileen.

"Thank you. Can you explain a little about the Rutherfords? Like why the castle is so empty? And why there aren't any visitors? There are a lot of things Lady Rutherford won't say, especially about Ewan. And I can't get a word out of him—about the inheritance situation. I hoped you'd, you know, shed some light. If it won't get you in trouble. The tea is great, by the way."

"There aren't many people the Rutherfords trust," Daphne said after a heavy pause. "They have almost no friends in town, for example. You saw the lady in her Bentley, right? That's how they are with outsiders: keep them at arm's length. To be honest, they barely speak to me these days. No one comes at Christmas or Easter. The laird, you see, wound up in that wheelchair as a result of an argument with a relative. So there's good reason for them to be cautious."

Eileen tapped her lip. "Why's Jenkins in the inner circle?"

"On Rowena's recommendation." Daphne rose from the table and began stacking a pile of dishes from the sink drainer. "They lost a butler some time ago and needed a replacement. Jenkins's references were provided by another titled couple. Seemed a good enough match, especially when he and the laird both liked rifles. Jenkins has never been keen on animals, though. Sort of squeamish it turns out when it comes to droppings."

Eileen considered her ruined ballet flats, the ones she'd worn on her first walk with Charlie so many weeks ago. "I can understand that."

"And the Rutherfords had no natural heir. Did you hear about that? Their two elder daughters moved to Canada and had no children. The will, as I heard it, allowed the estate to pass to the male next of kin, which would have been Ewan. But the lord cast him off on account of his father. Some ancient Scottish rule Lord Rutherfod researched allows him to name his next of kin himself if a break in marriage decorum makes the natural heir unfit. And Emily's marriage to a farmer, well, it didn't pass muster. So, as of a year ago, the new named heir is the lord's favorite servant, Earnest Jenkins, who'll pander to his every whim and change his bedpan but likely as not kick his corpse off the cliff as soon as he takes his last breath."

"Couldn't he have chosen someone better? I mean, Leven seems to be teeming with Rutherfords."

"If they had a claim, it would have gone to court. None have taken it that far, though. And none of them realize the wreck the estate is in. Its tax burden, its debts, and the upkeep, I tell you." She exhaled dramatically. "The family can't afford to mend the fence on their current earnings. Jenkins was a hero when he proved he could balance the books and extract more income for them here and there. They didn't even care when he skimmed off the top. If he was willing to take on the responsibility of the place and not carve it up into semi detached seaside bungalows, they were satisfied. Maybe not delighted but satisfied."

"So the girls"—Eileen nodded—"their daughters. They just got tired of the place?"

"Pretty much. The laird wasn't what you'd call a doting parent. He was a shouter when he still had his voice, a know-it-all. That attitude soured his children on the estate. By the time they were grown, they were totally uninterested in titles. Life in a draughty castle in coal country didn't appeal to them, no matter what coat of arms it came with. But Jenkins loves the tartan and all. I wouldn't be surprised if he had the laird's heraldry tattooed on his backside."

Eileen restarted her walk to the cave armed with scones and a thermos of hot tea. What an outpouring from Daphne. And that crack about a tattoo on Jenkins's backside! Thank God there was someone with a sense of humor at the castle, finally. It had been days since she'd heard anyone laugh and weeks since she'd heard a joke.

The fog was still clinging to tree limbs and hampered her view down the forest path. Branches snapped under her feet and her boots slipped on lichen. Reestablishing her footing, she followed the castle foundation and put her hand on the cliff face to keep secure contact. The stone meandered, cracks gave way to hollows, mildew changed to rivulets and moss. How many Rutherfords had come and gone in the span of just one crack? she wondered.

The wall fell away a moment later, and Eileen was at the cave. Inside, the fog cleared, but the darkness swallowed the daylight completely. Damn, she'd forgotten a flashlight. She searched her pockets and found her cell phone. A dim green light shone from it and allowed her to walk cautiously inside, holding the phone in front of her.

She didn't know what she was looking for, exactly. Some kind of message? A clue to the Temple-Hugh-Caedmon scandal? She got to the center of the cave, where the ceiling arched overhead and the piles of dirt heaped together. There were Emily's initials in yellow paint. Eileen held her phone to the walls. *Something's got to be down here.* Oops, she banged her head and dropped the phone.

"Ouch!" She rubbed the spot she'd hit. Where was that phone? It had dropped open, so she could still see a faint glimmer at her feet. She felt around with both hands. There it was. But what was wrapped around her phone? A swatch of fabric. She pulled at the material. It resisted. It was buried partly. She set the phone so it provided a more direct beam of light, grabbed hold of the dark cloth, and tugged hard.

It wasn't one piece of fabric but two, two long black gloves tied together at the ring finger. They looked like they'd been living down here for years. There were holes throughout the fabric. It was amazing there was anything left to them, at all.

"For my mother."

Eileen leaped up, her hand over her mouth. "Who's there?" She held her phone in front of her face, trying both to see in the dark and shield herself from whoever was approaching.

"You know."

Yes, Eileen did know. "Emily?"

"Take the gloves to my mother, Eileen." Emily's ghost emerged from a corner of the cave. She was still in the U2 T-shirt and combat boots. But she no longer wore her opera gloves. "Mother's mourned too long. These will show her it's almost over."

The ghost looked tired. Weary, in fact. Like she'd been up for the last two weeks.

"What's over?" Eileen took a tiny step forward.

"The old guard. Only you, Eileen, can overthrow that imposter. But you need Ewan to help you. Get him to follow the trail. You're matching up all the pieces. He'll come around. You can persuade him."

"But, Emily...No one listens to me. When I talk about Jenkins, or you, or who's driving the Bentley, they say I'm paranoid. And Ewan doesn't even want his fortune. He thinks that disputing the inheritance will get his brothers in trouble. And Hugh's one beer away from the unemployment line..."

"The others will be fine," the ghost replied, raising her hand. Her skin where the gloves had once been was a remarkable pearl white. Like the inside of a seashell and so translucent Eileen could see right through her arms to the stones behind her. Emily's hair, which had looked fire red on those previous nights, was now a medium shade of pink, with fronds of green—like she'd been hauled up in a fishing net from the bay.

"It's your choice. But you're the only one I have left, Eileen. Will you try?"

She nodded. And as she did so, the ghost smiled a tiny smile and faded into the far reaches of the cave. As she did so, she whispered, "The needle points the way."

Twenty-Two

Eileen ran flat out toward the farm, stumbling in the dense fog. *Careful of the bull*, she coached herself. It would be easy to take the wrong path in this weather.

The needle points the way. Eileen had seen only one needle since her arrival to Scotland. In Mr. Temple's curio cabinet.

There was another figure ahead. At first, it was just a blob amid the foliage. But then a man emerged. He wore a hooded raincoat, which blew out behind him in a gust of wind.

Hugh.

Was he the cowman, the drunkard, or the highwayman? Something moved in the grass behind him, but she couldn't see in the shadows.

"Eileen!" the figure yelled.

She didn't wait to see his face. She ran toward a thicket of holly.

"Eileen, wait!" The figure shouted. Then there was panting and a bark. Eileen turned.

"Charlie! Ewan! Thank God!"

"Ewan, thank God!"

He approached Eileen and removed the hood of his raincoat. "Are you all right?" Charlie leaped toward her, licking her face. She sank to the ground in relief.

"What's going on, Eileen?" He dropped to one knee. "What scared you so bad?"

"I thought...you looked like..."

"Fog's tricky, innit? I thought you were a banshee the way you were carryin' on. Where've you been, anyway? I looked for you at the Red House. You're covered in clay, you know."

She pulled Emily's gloves from her pocket. "I found these in the cave."

Ewan leaned toward the gloves, but he didn't touch them.

"Do you know whose they are?" she asked.

"They were hers." He looked away.

"Ewan." She frowned. "I thought you'd be, I don't know, excited that I found these." How to proceed? Anything she said about ghosts right now or the Rutherford inheritance was going to sound crazy or paranoid or both. Emily had recruited her and a summons from the dead couldn't be ignored. She'd come too far to back out. "Your mother, Ewan. She gave the gloves to me. She's visited me three times. You must have known her ghost was on the estate, right? Even my mother knows."

Ewan ran his hands through Charlie's fur.

"Ewan, I just told you your mother's ghost has been haunting me. Isn't that worth discussing? And don't you even want to hold her gloves? They've been buried in a cave. Her mission should interest you a little?"

"And what does she want, exactly?" he said.

"What is your deal? I mean, look, I've been touched by the after-life. By *your* mother. That gets you a spot on Oprah where I come from. You're acting like I've handed you a parking ticket."

Ewan sat down on the grass with a thump, his expression darkened, his mouth set. "She plays favorites, Eileen. All the Rutherfords do. I wouldn't confront Jenkins, so, yes, her ghost came to me, to persuade me to insist on my birthright. She told me if I wouldn't stick up for the Stalkers, she'd find someone who would. She didn't come back to the farm after that."

"How long ago was that?"

"Three years? Maybe more."

"So when she said she'd 'find someone who would,' she knew I'd be coming?"

"She said someone would come. She had that kind of foresight. Someone would come from outside." Ewan turned over a pinecone in

140

his hands, then threw it in a wide arc across the grass. "Haunting me wasn't productive. What could I do, you know? I was a kid, and at thirteen, no one listens."

"I'd listen."

"Well, sure, but who'd believe you? You think you're seeing ghosts."

"Why do you think she stopped coming to you?"

"Figured you'd be able to tell *me* that."

Eileen looked at her hands. "Back there in the cave, she said you'd given up and that I'd be able to help you." Eileen hesitated. "I think I'm supposed to protect you."

"From?"

"Look, she knew I'd found a syringe in Temple's cottage. The one I sent you a picture of. She said 'the needle points the way.'"

"I compared your syringe pictures to the type Hugh's got."

"And?"

"The one you found is for husbandry, that's for sure. The bore size matches what my brother uses to sedate the animals."

"Why does Hugh have to do that?"

"If the livestock are nervous or need surgery. The syringe type you found is used mostly for tranquilizer. It's rare for a professionally trained bull to need it at competition, but in Caedmon's case, it happens. It's legal to sedate at shows with a vet's prescription."

"How much does he get?"

"A *full* syringe of the size you found would put Caedmon to sleep three times over. Now if someone filled it with a steroid, like that Animal X, it would turn an uncastrated animal into a total monster."

"So, we have Mr. Temple helping himself to syringes from your brother's stash. We have Jenkins hurling insults at you at the games. We have Hugh, drunk and disorderly after a doping charge at competition, and we have a mysteriously wound-up, charging bull. We also have Emily warning me to keep you out of danger and a careening Bentley almost mowing us down. Don't you feel a little uncomfortable with all that? A little, I don't know, marked?"

He picked up a daisy from the lawn and set it gently behind Eileen's ear. As his knuckles brushed her cheek, her chest caught. "Emily was into conspiracies, too. She was always peeling back the layers. But I'm not like her that way. It's not my responsibility to show people the error of their ways. If I took the inheritance, like she wanted, it would be to steady the boat, not turn it upside down."

Eileen nodded vigorously. "Of course. So, you looking for a sidekick or what? You know I'm going to investigate this syringe/bull/inheritance scenario anyway. I'm a meddler. You want double billing?"

He looked at the sky. "Do I have a choice?"

"No." She smiled.

"Your show, detective." He placed a butterfly kiss on Eileen's nose. "But let's do it quietly, OK? No more snooping in the village."

Eileen raised her hand in mock salute.

"And you can leave Hugh out of it."

"But, Ewan, how can he be innocent?" She understood his urge to protect his brother, but she couldn't overlook such an obvious villain. Those angry sneers, the menacing behavior even toward Granny. Hugh remained the best candidate to rain down disaster on the estate. He had the motive to do something like run them over in the car—jealously and resentment; he had the means—access to Mr. Temple's Bentley keys; and he had the opportunity—disappearing from the games parking lot with enough time to get behind the wheel that night. He also had a secondary weapon, an angry bull, if someone got in his way. Like Emily had.

"Hugh needs the job," Ewan said evenly. "He's decent. And he has nowhere else to go. If you want me involved, leave Hugh out of it, love." With that, Ewan stood up. He didn't look at Eileen for a moment. He regarded the horizon, stuck a hand in his pocket and jangled a set of keys. Then he turned a skeptical look back at her. "You got my attention with the syringe. And now if Emily's back..." He trailed off. "We'll investigate after the summer sheering, OK? It'll be a few days."

The fog was lifting now. It hovered eight feet above the earth, dense and swirling, still, like steam rising from a cauldron. Ewan kissed Eileen lightly on the mouth, but just as she started to lean in to him, he pulled away, offsetting her balance.

He moved a little like Charlie, she realized. Sort of zigzagging and nonspecific. Almost like a bee. Several days were an awfully long time to wait. But she had finally made a breakthrough. He'd agreed to investigate his family's dispute. Even if he didn't want the lord's title, the idea might grow on him if she helped him. Man, if I were due a castle, she thought, I'd have my bags packed within the hour.

Twenty-Three

The next few days dragged like flooded boots. Eileen looked for Ewan on the hillside and along the forest path. All she found, besides his infinite free-range sheep were puffy clouds, loitering and unhurried. Emily's mission would have to wait. There wasn't a thing more to do while Ewan sheared sheep.

Things with Rowena got tense. Eileen's constant questions about Jenkins put her on edge. She was snappish and slammed doors.

Eileen followed right in step. "It's a radio, not a wireless. Why would anyone call a three-day weekend a bank holiday?"

Joyce tried to lighten the mood. "Let's tour a distillery. How 'bout trying blood pudding?" She was trying.

Nothing pleased Rowena any more. Eileen knew she'd aired too many opinions at the castle, inadvertently reminding Lady Rutherford of Rowena's role in Jenkins's hire.

"I know!" Eileen howled at a third reminder to get the mail. "I'm not the bloody butler, I'm getting to it."

"Well, at least clean up after yourself." Rowena eyed the open door of the bathroom, where Eileen had left a carpet of towels.

The irritation stream was constant.

"The front door's unlocked."

"Charlie wasn't fed."

"Kitchen light's still on."

"You left your bed unmade."

After two days of the same, Eileen cast her white flag. "I know you're mad I brought up Jenkins's history at the castle. And I'm sorry. But you don't have to hang me with it."

"I may not be welcome in the castle for another ten years, but never mind."

"Well, I can see how you and Jenkins would be friends! You're both so sure you're right all the time."

"I am nothing like Earnest Jenkins," she answered darkly.

"Really?" Eileen's hands went to her waist. "Why not?"

"Just tell her," Granny said over the top of her paper.

"Because!" Rowena snapped her book shut. "He's a common hired man who saw an opportunity. And after Emily broke with the family, he's the one person who'll mind them. He's not entitled and he's not Scottish but he's the lord's heir. No one likes it, but there we are."

"Does Lady Rutherford like it?" Eileen asked.

"What do you think?"

"Easy, now." Joyce crossed the room with a tray of silver. She sat on the floor and began to polish it next to the window. "Eileen's sixteen, remember?" Joyce looked at Rowena over a silver ladle. "She has a romantic imagination, but she's not unreasonable. She asks questions, even at questionable times. Jenkins is a con man, pure and simple. He conned you, and now he's conning them. At least they get their baths drawn for them by someone in nice clothes."

Rowena sat down hard next to Charlie on the couch. "Well, since you're so keen to know, he also saved the laird's life. He found him, senseless, at the bottom of the cliff, and revived him. He'd been pushed over the bluff by Hugh, people think. Broke seven vertebrae."

"Well..." Eileen knit her hands together. "That's heroic, I'll admit. But enough to earn a family fortune? The guy lectured *me* about being an outsider, and all the while he's no one and a freeloader."

"You can imagine the talk in Leven. But Rutherford made it official." Rowena shrugged. "So the con man will do what he likes. Unless he breaks the law. Jail time might leave a real slight on the Rutherfords."

"Can the laird even voice an opinion?" Joyce asked. "Is he mentally sound?"

"He says a little. Now and then." Rowena nodded. "I've seen his signature since the accident. It's a little wild but legible."

Rowena seemed in better spirits now that she was unloading the saga. She scruffed Charlie's neck and made the first smile Eileen had seen in a week. "Jenkins was well suited to the elderly when I met him in Northumberland, so I recommended him for the Rutherfords' post. And, since none of his book-cooking had come to light and I liked what I saw at my school friend's house, I made the introduction."

"But you didn't tell him about Emily being disowned?" Eileen pressed. "Or a will in dispute?"

"I may have mentioned some arguments."

"Oh, Rowena." Fran shook her head.

She held her hands in surrender. "He would have found out anyway, the moment he interviewed. There was no reason to think he'd swindle them. He was a complete professional down south. With fewer airs, that's for sure. And boots polished, dogs fed, bills paid. He was an excellent butler but 'due for a change,' as he put it."

"And did he embezzle from your friends?" Eileen asked.

"Rowena?" Joyce insisted.

"Well, as it turns out..."

Fran winced.

Rowena fretted with her necklace. "But *I* never knew 'til after. He'd been on the job two years here before that scandal broke. I think Clyde showed me the article. Anyway, Jenkins was well installed. The lord had had his fall, conferred decisions on him. It was too late to do anything."

"But hold on." Eileen stood from her chair. "Everyone knew he was a crook, and the Rutherfords made him heir, anyway?"

"The laird flew over that cliff. Lady R. worried his temper would worsen to cruelty with those injuries. Jenkins softened him! Of course it was still a shock when he got written into the will, but in a way, we were grateful for him."

There was quiet in the living room. A yew branch snatched at the window. A sheep baaed.

"I was a fool." Rowena lowered her head. She let a hand fall to her side, pale and small.

Eileen wanted to reach out to Rowena. She'd never seen her like this.

"He seemed so competent," Rowena said in a near whisper. "So reliable. And goodness they needed him. The lady alone with the entire estate, the tenants, the animal permits, the lord's pills. Jenkins excelled at all those things."

"What a prince," Eileen murmured.

"And we'll answer to him soon," Granny added.

Rowena walked to the water pitcher sitting on an end table and poured herself a drink. "The will can't be undone 'cept by the Lord himself."

There being no chance anymore to lighten the mood, Eileen grabbed the dog leash. "Charlie, let's get some air."

She had to find Ewan, light a fire under him. The sheering could wait a day, but Jenkins couldn't get away with this. He just couldn't.

From the hilltop, Eileen could usually tell if the Stalkers were busy. If the sheering was over, she'd march right down there. Already she'd waited four days without contact. There was only so long a girl could hold out. And, jeez, didn't he miss her?

She had a speech in mind, or snatches of one: *All the while Jenkins was skimming off the top!* But before she could rehearse the lines, her phone rang. *Finally.*

"Hello?"

"Eileen?"

"Ewan!"

"There's something you should see, Eileen. Meet me in the barn."

Twenty-Four

The wind was up. Eileen pulled her hood over her head and tied it with the draw string and stuffed her hands into her pockets. Charlie pulled off his leash.

"Charlie, your timing..."

He darted off weaving through barley stalks, then doubled back and bounced at her heels. His hair was full of the usual burrs and bristles. Today he'd latched onto a particularly mean-looking thistle. It had a fluffy purple flower like a ball of goose down and some awful-looking thorns. They stung as Eileen tried to remove them, and he pawed mournfully at the ear where they clung.

"Poor boy!"

Suddenly Charlie drew back from Eileen. He showed his teeth and growled. Eileen turned in the direction he was looking. A pounding noise was approaching. It vibrated the nearby leaves, the very air. In its wake, barley stalks flew.

Though her view was obscured by the grain, Eileen knew what was coming. Hoof beats, heavy breaths. Charlie backed into the barley and disappeared.

"Wait!" Where had he gone? The barley trembled in every direction. She tore her phone out of her pocket but her hands were shaking so badly she couldn't press the keys. So she ran toward the castle, the same direction she'd seen Charlie go.

"Help! The bull's out! Ewan, someone!"

The closer she got to the castle, the safer she would be. Right? Caedmon would pull up, retreat. Someone would put his leash back on.

But the hoof beats didn't retreat. Nor the awful panting.

Her progress was fast but erratic. She ran toward the farm, then turned sharply uphill, then tripped over a fallen branch. She righted herself and shouldered into thick brambles.

When the castle came into view, the hooves seemed quieter. She stood up part way, peering through the barley to see if Caedmon had followed. But then out of nowhere, she was falling.

She found herself in almost total darkness. In a well? A rabbit hole? She braced herself against a savage pain in her hip. She'd fallen well landing on her side, just above her hip, with the majority of shock absorbed in the tissue and not the bone. Still, the angle of the fall had been severe. Her entire left side throbbed.

She tried to stand. That hurt, a lot. But she could do it. She hobbled to the edge of the shaft and braced herself against the earthen wall. What was this—Middle Earth? She'd escaped one danger aboveground only to find something worse below. The light above was visible but faint. Could be a coalmine service tunnel. She prayed it wasn't prone to cave-in.

Eileen felt the prickle of sweat at her armpit. Her throat scratched like sandpaper. *Don't panic.* She surveyed the walls. Gritty, irregular earthen sides about five feet across, depth, some thirty feet, wet soil with small pebbles, nearby dripping sound. Maybe there was a ladder somewhere as an escape from this kind of fall. Mine accidents happened all the time, so, ladders, right? She ran her hands over the damp walls digging her fingers into the earth. But she didn't find any metal. Her hands came away with chunks of dirt and a little moss. Lucky the shaft wasn't full of water. Regardless, climbing out was not an option.

Phone. If it was still charged, she had a lifeline. She pulled the iPhone out of her pocket and held it as high as she could toward the light at the opening of the shaft, then pushed the speed-dial number for Ewan. It rang and rang and rang.

"You've reached Ewan Stalker. I'm out with the sheep. Leave a message if you want. Beep."

Shit.

"Ewan, I've fallen down a mine shaft in some barley field. Hurry. I hear these things collapse." She clicked the phone off.

So here were the facts: She'd been chased into a hole by the bull. The bull had no business in a barley field. And furthermore, someone ought to seal this outrageous hole in the middle of an open field. Maybe it had been opened for her to fall in. That was it! She was the pinball being chased. Fifty points to Temple or Hugh who had prepped Caedmon for the charge. They'd been a little careless, though. She'd survived. Now if she could just get out of here, she'd squeal on both of them.

She sank onto the floor, easing her back side slowly downward. That hurt. And there was something sharp poking in her back. She swiveled to remove whatever it was. It was wedged in tight, though. There was a little shine on its surface revealing a regular shape, circular or oval, sticking out of the side of the tunnel wall. Having nothing better to do, she began to free it.

She dug a trench around one side where the earth was porous and came away easily. There was more rock and sand on the other side, so Eileen set to it with a ballpoint pen she found swimming in her pocket. Within a few minutes, she'd freed two -thirds of her treasure. Levering with the ballpoint, she dislodged the stone with a pop and flung it across the cavern onto the wet sand.

Having seen the collector's piece, Eileen was fairly sure this was a rune. It was the same shape and size as Temple's, only where his version was chipped at the edge, this was whole. It had the same bull outline as the one Eileen had held, but where she wiped the mud away, this carving was much deeper cut. Its creator had carved a very dainty animal, its horns curved over its head in a heart formation, the shaggy hair hanging down between its forefeet like a beard. Its profile was determined, and though the shoulders showed obvious strength, violence, even, it wore a ring in its nose with a lead rope attached.

The tail of this creature curled up over its back like Temple's carving had, with a tuft of hair at the end erupting in four directions, like from a fountain. No question what that image brought to mind. This must be an amulet of male power. Eileen wondered if it was meant as a gift or a totem against bad luck. It was crosshatched on the back side with foreign markings, a slogan perhaps or password, maybe even the artist's name. What would this be worth? A month's salary? A farmhouse? A tribal estate?

Eileen put the stone slowly into her coat pocket, where it rested cold against her hip. She wondered if that's how the first owner carried it around. It was heavy, two to three pounds, and it could pack a wallop from a sling shot if someone got too close on an Iron Age night.

Overhead Eileen heard a rustling. She held the stone close and scrunched her body against the wall. If it was the bull master, come to finish her off, she'd stay well out of view. The rustling sound turned into a snuffle, though, and a furry head popped over the aperture.

"Charlie!" Eileen waved. "Good dog! Go get help. Get Ewan. Go boy. Go to the farm!"

Charlie barked, wagged his tail and bounded away.

Now the waiting. And it could be a while. Charlie had spent a good half day stalking an abandoned bee hive a few week ago. Finding Ewan might involve the same detours.

But the look on his face when she showed the rune to him! He'd be amazed. And proud! This must be the artifact Jenkins had been digging for all this time. Temple believed it existed on the estate, the archaeologists from London did. But check it out—a Yank visitor had found it on her own. And...God. This was the very trinket Emily had died for, failing to give it over to the man in control of the bull. It was a treasure with a curse attached, for sure. Not the kind of thing you wanted on you very long.

A noise jerked Eileen's attention upward: jangling keys.

"Ewan! Thank God. Throw something down! I can't climb but maybe you can pull me."

"Be there in a mo, dear." It wasn't Ewan. It was Temple. And he wasn't with Charlie. Eileen felt a wave of nausea. How did Temple know she was in this shaft? He was fastening ropes overhead. He was lowering something. This wasn't good. He'd finish her off with a collectable dagger.

"Hi, er, Mr. Temple. What are you doing up there?"

"I'm here to rescue you, what else? I can lower meself down or hoist you up. It happens to lambs all the time, you'll be glad to know. You're not the only—well, you *are* the only lass this has happened to. But not the only lost lamb." He chuckled again.

"Uh, I'd rather wait." Eileen twisted her jacket zipper. Keep clear of him. He'd take the stone. He'd tie her up with those ropes, she was sure of it.

"Wait?" Temple said, astonished. "Wait for what?"

She still hadn't seen Temple's face, but she could hear him assembling something overhead. Something with crampons and sharp corners. She shuddered.

"You're still injured," she shouted up at him. "Get Ewan to hoist me up."

"Och, lass. If you go waitin' for your true love every time...Oi, Ewan. Didn't see you there. I was just about..."

Eileen almost puked for relief. In twenty minutes, she was out. Ewan took hold of Temple's gear and lowered himself to her on a rope and cage assembly, then brought her back up via pulley. It was all very *Coal Miner's Daughter.*

"How did Temple know where I was?" Eileen asked half an hour later with a mug of tea at the farmhouse.

"I was wondering that, too." Ewan stroked her hair. He'd thrown a comforter around her and stoked the fire. She'd refused Dr. Marshall. *Something fishy with that guy.* "Charlie found me. But I don't know how Temple got your whereabouts. Or how you fell down that shaft in the first place."

"The bull chased me." Eileen set her tea down.

"What?"

She nodded. "He charged me, Ewan. He was loose in the barley field and went for me. I ran every which way to lose him, wound up tripping and falling in that hole. I'm sure Temple saw the whole thing—planned the whole thing. He arrived much too quickly for it to have been spontaneous. It *was* him provoking the stampedes."

"Eileen—that wasn't Caedmon in the barley." He poured Eileen more tea. "He's been at the vet since nine this morning."

"How do you know?" she struggled to say.

"I helped Hugh board him into the trailer this morning."

"But you didn't see him come back, did you?"

"He's still there, love."

"But..."

"Could have been a grouse in the field or a hare."

"Ewan." She raked a hand through her hair. Her hands smelled of coal. They trembled visibly. "Something chased me."

"It's all right, lass."

What was he, coddling her? "I didn't imagine it."

"You've heard a lot of stories. A lot of things could sound like a stampeding bull. And there was that careening car. It's understandable."

She crossed her arms.

"All I'm saying is that whatever chased you might also have been one of the staff. Someone in a farm vehicle. You said Temple appeared awfully fast at the top of that shaft. It could have been him with a mower or combine, winding you up—herding you into that hole. What worries me worse is the fact that the shaft was sealed until today. Sealed with a steel cover and a blowtorch. There's no reason it should have been reopened. And if anyone would have known about it, the gardener of the estate would."

"Would he also know about this?" Eileen brought out her rune and set it with a thump on his kitchen table. Against the unpainted wood, it looked like an old gray meat loaf outlined with a bull design.

"Where did you find *that*?" He reached to touch the stone, his hand trembling.

"At the bottom of the mine shaft. Think it's what the archaeologists were looking for?"

Ewan followed the design with his finger and nodded. "This has been on the list of missing world heritage objects for seventy-five years. It was considered pillaged by the English, like the Stone of Scone. They stole everything from us, down to the last little pebble. This was reclaimed by some Rutherford in one of the Highland wars and, they say, got reburied to save it from another future looting. The archaeologists got an anonymous tip that it was on the estate. But they were just..."

"Digging in the wrong place."

"What do we do with it?" Eileen leaned toward him.

"For now, keep it hidden."

Twenty-Five

Ewan helped Eileen into the yellow pickup. She'd be sore for a few days from her fall, but she wasn't concussed or bleeding. It was time to get back to the Red House and face the ladies.

The Red House seemed also the best place for their artifact, under Eileen's mattress, at least to start. Now they had to figure out what to do about Mr. Temple. Accuse him, call the cops, blackmail a confession from him about deliberately hurting Eileen. Whichever way they went, Eileen had to face the music with Joyce, get grounded, do the penance. She'd settle up there and then get back to resolving the Rutherford mystery.

Ewan had just turned over the engine of the truck when Charlie started to bark.

Eileen turned to see what was bothering him. "Oh, Mr. Jenkins." She averted her eyes. Now was not the time to start a fight.

Ewan bristled visibly in his seat and turned off the engine. He got out of the car, walked around the front, and placed himself firmly in front of Eileen's door.

Jenkins's approach was from the castle. He looked different today, not his usual Geek Squad, more madman in the attic. His hair was sticking up on one side like he'd been suctioned with a vacuum. His arms and torso were covered in earth. His tie was undone, and one of his pockets hung inside out. The one familiar item was his tartan jacket. His eyes cast thunder. He looked angry enough right then to throw something.

Eileen looked between the two men and lowered her window. "Uh, that's the Rutherford tartan, right?"

"The very one." But he wasn't looking at Eileen. He stared contemptuously at Ewan. For someone who'd just been in a street fight or whatever, he spoke very calmly. "We've had this tartan for generations in my clan."

Ewan didn't even look at the kilt. "So it's a Jenkins tartan?"

"You should know, as the grandchild of the family, that's it's the Rutherford tartan. The heir's tartan. One you're not entitled to, I should add."

"In case you hadn't noticed, butler, you're on my farm. This is Stalker property, clearly stated in the Rutherfords' land grant, and you're trespassing."

Jenkins was about to speak when a voice came from the barn. A voice of alarm.

"Jenkins!"

Hugh was running to them, breathless in an unsteady jog. "Where's Temple? He was supposed to meet me." Hugh looked pretty rough, too, Eileen noticed. His eyes were redder than usual and his skin was, well, nasty—like he hadn't slept in three nights. His rain poncho flapped around his shoulders, and a smear of dirt marked one shoulder.

"Caedmon's on a rampage." Hugh turned narrow eyes on Jenkins. "Did you send Temple to raid my equipment? I'm missing a..." But there Hugh noticed Eileen, still inside the truck. "Ewan, what's *she* doing here? Don't we have enough trouble?"

"Eileen's just had an accident in one of our fields. She may have broken a rib, though she won't let me call Dr. Marshall. Temple's got a lot to answer for today. It was an open mine shaft she fell in."

Hugh rubbed his head and actually looked a little sorry for Eileen at that instant.

Jenkins scowled. "We're managing fine, Hugh. You can push off."

"Jenkins. If you provoke me today, so help me God—"

"I'm taking Eileen back to the Red House," Ewan interrupted. He walked back to the driver's door. "If you want Temple, he's probably packing. I asked Granny to sack him for negligence, leaving a mine shaft unsealed. Try at his cottage if you want him. It's where Eileen found your syringe, by the way—in his art collection. I'd wager he's moved it by now, of course. Your mate's the number one suspect behind Caedmon's wild streak."

The man's jaw dropped. Hugh looked at Jenkins. He looked at Eileen. "Jesus, Mary, and Joseph."

Jenkins ran his hand through his hair. "This isn't going to go well for the estate."

"Shut up!" Eileen shouted. She'd been waiting weeks to say that to him. "No one here's gonna call you Lord Rutherford, OK? I don't care what kilt you're wearing."

"Oi, nice one." Ewan gunned the engine and peeled out of the farmyard.

When they arrived at the Red House, Ewan put the engine in neutral and threw an arm around Eileen. "You didn't think I was gonna say anything about the syringe, did you?"

She shook her head.

"I knew Jenkins had been up to something. But I thought we'd better have more evidence before we laid it on the table. Then when you found and needle *and* doping material and a rune, there was obviously no way to keep quiet or to shut you up." He stroked her cheek.

"Nope, not a chance."

"Rural people, you see, we don't change. But you heap enough shit on us we eventually react."

"I won't heap shit, I promise!"

"And I swore I'd never take anything from my grandparents." He looked at the castle. "They stripped the Stalkers of everything. I got shipped off to school, Hugh hit the bottle, Danny stopped talking. And the way Jenkins spun it, I had abandoned my post."

"You were a child when the lord had his accident. You'd already lost two parents. It was a rifle backfire. How were you responsible for that?"

"I'll always be responsible," Ewan whispered. Then he tightened jaw and reached for her hand. "C'mon, girl." They'd been sitting on the drive already ten minutes. "You gonna brandish that weird rune and help me get my life back?"

She snuggled closer to him. Their lips met, briefly, then hungrily. Finally. What a girl had to do around here.

It wasn't a long kiss, though. "Any protective old ladies in those windows?" Ewan asked, separating from Eileen.

"Plenty," Eileen said. "Need one?"

"Got my own, thanks. So, we've got work to do."

"What's first?"

"Watching Caedmon to see if anyone unusual's hanging aboot."

"A stakeout." She grinned.

"Just like the movies." He squeezed her hand.

"How 'bout if I follow Hugh?"

His hand slackened at that. "You still think he's the villain?"

"He *is* Caedmon's handler." Before she could go on, though, Ewan got out of the car and swung Eileen's door wide.

"I have work. And I'm sure you're needed at home."

"But..." She stepped reluctantly onto the drive. "Our plan."

"For *my* future. Yes, there was a plan. But charging my brother with attempted murder is not part of it. I spent the last five years getting him job security, so I'm not going to help you get him arrested just because you saw him drunk."

"But, Ewan, look at the facts. He's in charge of a violent animal who's known to be wreaking havoc. He was abandoned by his father. He's harassed constantly by Jenkins. You don't see how he's a powder keg? Caedmon's an awful big bull in the hands of a very bitter man."

Ewan tightened his lips.

"They're using you." She started slowly toward the Red House, but then stopped and reached for his hand. "No, don't back away. You told me you would face facts, so here they are: Temple either stole that syringe or got it directly from Hugh to dope an animal, or a person, even. He learned from your brother how manipulate Caedmon to stampede pedestrians. That, or he's using farm equipment, like you said, to scare people: me, Emily, who's next? My granny? What if Hugh is training the bull to act out his revenge on Lord Rutherford? Do you know what he's capable of? Ewan, he is your big brother. Someone who's supposed to protect *you*. Imagine the humiliation of having to answer to you when you're twelve years younger than him. Imagine the rage every time he thinks of his father leaving him for Emily. Of you, not him, getting visits from the castle. Of you being sent to private school. Anger like that changes a person. For all you know"—she sighed—"Hugh may even think he's entitled to some of the family inheritance!"

"What?" Ewan tore his hand out of Eileen's. "Hugh's not even related to the Rutherfords. He's just the kid off some drunk farmer."

She sucked her breath. "I'm not telling you anything you haven't already considered."

He wouldn't listen. He hurled himself in the car.

"Everything all right?" Joyce said. She *had* been watching.

Eileen wished she could take back her rampage. But it was too late. Ewan roared off, his pickup soon no bigger than an angry bee upon the hillside.

Would he come back? Was she wrong to have let loose like that? What else was there to do? She could no longer keep the thoughts bottled up. She had about as much chance at holding her peace as Rowena did joining the silent nuns' order.

Twenty-Six

Yeah, Ewan was annoyed. He hadn't called in three days, and then it dragged to five. Things would work out, though. They had to. Eileen had shocked the sense into him. Insulted his family, maybe, harassed him, but what else was there to do? People were falling into abandoned mines while he dallied. At least she had the gloves and the rune to show for. Without them, she'd come off as kinda crazy.

She did have to admit she'd been a little shrewish, a little righty-right. She'd never insisted like that, but she'd never had this kind of axe to grind. With Ewan's future in tatters, it was a serious problem to solve. And she wasn't getting sidelined with three would-be assassins at large.

If Ewan wouldn't help, Eileen would go on alone. She did have to get that Animal X, though. The syringe on its own wasn't proof of much and it wasn't going to be easy to get back into Temple's house, especially if she had indirectly gotten him fired. She'd also just been grounded.

"We told you to stay out of their affairs!" Joyce shrieked when Eileen returned bruised and covered in mine debris. And though a quick X-ray at Kirkaldy Casualty showed the injuries to be little more than bruising, her mom made the new rules very clear: "You will stay at the Red House for the remainder of the summer. Period, full stop."

She did some family albums, and she took the recommended rest and one or two pain meds. She folded sheets, fluffed pillows. Ewan finally called, but Eileen wasn't allowed to use the phone unsupervised. "He's brought this out in you, you know," Rowena whispered after Joyce hid her iPhone. "You snoop worse than I do."

Try as she might, though, Joyce could not separate a teenager from her cell phone for long. Eileen found it in the clothes hamper and hid it in her jogging belt.

Six days after her fall, she was allowed out. Rowena had taken Fran to a rose show, Joyce was dead on her feet from doing most of Eileen's heavy chores, and when Clyde stopped in to tell them about the newly laid eggs the Stalkers were giving away, Joyce finally gave into a furlough. "If it'll stop your constant sighing, go get a dozen eggs. But if you're not back in one hour, I'm coming over. And you know I'll do something embarrassing."

Once more, she passed the little potting shed/greenhouse where Jenkins liked to dig. There was a considerable mess inside. She hadn't remembered such disorder when she passed before, but it truly looked like it had been looted. The door was hanging on its hinge and inside everything was upside down. Had Temple trashed it in a rage against his boss? Jenkins did sign the checks, after all.

There was a rustle in the path-side brush. Eileen shrank low. She didn't have Charlie, it could be him. But no, it was the man himself, Earnest Jenkins. Eileen ducked behind a pile of flowerpots and garden tools. Something dripped nearby, creating a rank smell, like diesel fuel. Eileen pulled her turtleneck up around her face. Around the flower pots, she could see Jenkins digging among small trees. After making some progress, he set the spade down, leaned on it, and muttered to himself.

"Stupid cow...know-it-all...and that useless bloody soak..." His disoriented string of insults continued a good few minutes while he pounded at the earth. Finally, a metallic *pong* sounded off the edge of his spade. "About bloody time!" He tossed the spade aside and dug in with both hands.

Eileen stood for a better look. Jenkins had withdrawn something from the hole. It wasn't large, about the size of his palm, grayish, oval, flat. *Another* rune! That made three. Were any of them real? With all the effort he'd spent here, Jenkins clearly thought his was genuine.

She took a step closer but awkwardly. Her boot caught something, the strap of a messenger bag. She maneuvered clear of it but dragged the flap open by mistake. A green spiral notebook came into view along with a stack of letters bundled with a rubber band. Next to the letters was a yellow liquid in an industrial-sized pharmacy bottle. Checking that Jenkins wasn't looking, she bent down to take a closer look: *Animal X*. With great care, Eileen pocketed the vial and with just a second's hesitation slid the spiral notebook and parcel of letters out of the messenger bag and into the lining of her anorak. Then she zipped her coat and slunk into the trees.

A crack in the undergrowth stopped her instantly. "Happy hunting?"

Damn it. Eileen straightened to her full height and turned to face him. He was leaning against the potting shed door and dusting the earth from his hands.

"And you?" She let her hands fall to her sides. "Find what you were looking for?"

"It's my land. I do what I please. But you"—he gestured toward at his messenger bag—"you've picked the wrong pocket. You think you can just do as you please. You put the snow on the old lady, sure enough. But what I'd like to know is who exactly you think you are? These"—he indicated his looted belongings—"are private. And they're things I've earned. Seems to me, Ms. Morgan of Evanston, Illinois, you don't know the meaning of that term, where you come from. You have no land or titles. So why are you meddling?"

Jenkins started pacing, like the show animals at the Fife games. Eileen lowered her gaze, attempting to look forlorn. Without adjusting her gaze she felt for her phone and hit the 3 button that speed-dialed Ewan and cranked up the volume to its highest setting.

"You're right," she said, trying to keep the shake out of her voice. "I'm a meddler. I'm in a family of meddlers." As she said this, she stuck her left hand in her pocket, feeling the Animal X bottle. She very slowly removed it and positioned the vial behind her back. There, with the aid of her right hand, she undid the childproof cap and spilled a few drops into the lining of her jacket.

"Well, here on the estate meddling has its penalties. I'd hoped to let you off with a little scare. You walked away from the Bentley, as I planned. But when you kept nosing around, Temple reminded me of the abandoned service entrance to the mine. But Rowena's dog dragged Stalker over to fish you out. Temple's no use anymore."

"What did you bribe him with?" Since she was piping the conversation directly to Ewan's voice mail, she wanted on record who had done what, in what order. The playback from Verizon would vindicate her fraud theory once and for all.

"I don't see that it matters, but he got a rune stone. Know what that is?"

"Not really." Sounded like Jenkins had himself an entire rock garden of fake carvings. Seeing as Temple thought his first rune, back in the curio cabinet, was a forgery, he probably believed Jenkins had paid him off with a real treasure. But who, now, would ever know?

"You saw the curio cabinets." Jenkins eyed her. "Yes, Temple mentioned it. His stone was a good forgery, like most of his collection. It's hard be sure what's real, isn't it? Who's the man he says he is." He picked flecks of dirt from his fingernail. "Who's the shadow in the night."

"I assume you stole that." She nodded at Temple's coat pocket where he'd stashed his carving. "And the steroids. You took them from the veterinarian supply and pumped them into Caedmon. Then he lost at competition and made Hugh look incompetent, plus he was ready to stampede the whole county after the dose you gave him."

"Oh, the imagination of the young!" Jenkins feigned surprise. "But you are correct. I even built a remote-control bull—to scare trespassers. It's on skis, rides a rail, not very convincing until there's fog, but then... watch out."

"And Temple isn't much of an accomplice. He lost focus and couldn't finish you off. Sappy windbag. Gave me an earful about Emily's death and all the mine tragedies. Man's completely superstitions. Was sure Emily was punishing him. He changed his tone, though, when I threatened his demented Mum. Took his payoff all quiet than. It's very nice, you know. His stone. Excellent workmanship for a forgery. I have a man in Brighton does amazing work." He clicked his tongue in satisfaction.

"Now you and I...right this way."

"Where?"

"In the shed. Now."

"I'm not going anywhere." Her hands started shaking.

"Well, don't say I didn't try to be reasonable." He brought a hunting rifle from behind his body. It was sort of antique-looking, with brass curly cues along the barrel. A showpiece from the lord's mantel, perhaps.

Eileen's throat made a crack, but she kept her poker face the best she could. "You gonna shoot me? Don't you think a rifle will be kinda loud?"

He fired a single shot overhead. Shards of wood flew from a tree a hundred yards away. Eileen's mouth fell open.

"That's what I thought." Jenkins poked her with the tip of the gun. "Move."

She made her way toward the open door he had been leaning against. He pulled it wider, the hinges squeaking as he did so. There was that bad smell again, combination car exhaust and litter box. Eileen's eyes watered.

"I'll take that bottle now."

She stopped a few feet inside the greenhouse. "What botle?"

He pointed the nose of the rifle at her ear.

"OK, OK! You can lower the gun!" She reached into her coat and handed him the steroids. The liquid she'd spilled in her coat lining should be enough for the narc guys to sample later on. "That stuff's cruel to animals. Wrecks their nervous system and their adrenals."

He appeared indignant at that remark. "For your information, this compound is saving the Rutherford dynasty. It's painless. Injected into fatty tissue to help a good animals become superb. Like his lordship. If I didn't give him his dose every night, he'd be comatose. I've wired both creatures so they can give a good show at the right moment."

Eileen's mouth fell open. "You're giving that to a man in a wheelchair! You're a monster."

"I'll ignore that," Jenkins said. "But so you know, competitive breeders have used steroids for years. So have athletes all over the States." He carefully inserted the steroid bottle back into his messenger bag. God, Eileen thought. Maybe he doped Hugh, too. She'd never known a guy lose his temper as quickly. Eileen had no idea anymore what Jenkins was capable of. He was after all a butler pointing a rifle.

Jenkins pushed her into the back of the shed and motioned her onto a pile of potting soil while he extracted items from the drawer of a moldy dresser. The earth Eileen sat on was covered with spider webs, and from the chew marks on the mulch bags, this was also home to several rodents. But there was something even stranger among the burlap sacks. Peeking from underneath them was the finger of a satin glove. It lay trapped under the mulch, mildewed and rotting, and two fingers were extended, like a buried person was still inside that glove, trying to escape the earth pile. Eileen leaned slowly toward the glove and yanked it out.

"What are these?" She turned to Jenkins. "Something you forgot to bury in your hole?"

Jenkins's face went slack, and he dropped a role of duct tape. "What did...I'm not going to...Look. I had nothing to do with Emily's death. She wasn't stampeded, not at my hand, anyway."

"And she didn't have a heart attack," Eileen whispered. She shouldn't know this, and yet she did. She understood what had happened in this place. Emily's last moments unrolled before her on the greenhouse glass like a 1940s newsreel. "She died here. In this building. She had that stone you just uncovered but wouldn't let you have it. So you killed her. Shot her up with *compound* and stopped her heart. Then dumped her in Caedmon's field, making it look like he'd rammed her."

A muscle in his neck twitched. He was cunning but still a coward. "You can't prove that!"

"Well, I can!" came a voice. Jenkins heard it, too. He staggered backward raising his rifle in alarm.

"Where are you?" He was afraid. He ran to his satchel but slammed his head against a hanging plant. "I've had enough out of you!" he rubbed his injured head. "I have my due! I'm entitled to something for all my work."

He took up his satchel from the floor, but spilled its contents onto his shoes.

Eileen slid toward a window that had lost its glass. Though occupied with his duffle, Jenkins did still have that gun. She'd need to be careful, but the moment of distraction was a good one. She dropped to her stomach and crawled through the broken window.

"Oh, no you don't!"

Jenkins slid a bullet into its chamber. The pain in Eileen's hip roared.

"Don't shoot!" she called back.

Instead, Jenkins grabbed at her disappearing body. She kicked for all she was worth, got a good thump onto his chest, but then an explosion. He fired his rifle, greenhouse glass shattered everywhere. Pain deafened her to whatever the man was shouting at her. Her hip had jammed against the window casing, and Jenkins was stamping on her, trying to crush the tendons in the back of her leg. Then he changed plans and sat on her. She yelped, but he was too heavy to remove.

"I could do this slowly, Eileen, slice your Achilles with one of these shards. Or I could tie Charlie in a tree, and let you watch him suffocate himself trying to get down. Then there's your mother, with that weakness for shortbread."

"Don't touch them," Eileen hissed.

"Why not? I have keys to the Red House. My agent is already in their vegetable plot. And it's not the first time I..."

He was cut off by a scream. His own scream followed by a thud. The weight on Eileen's leg lifted. She heaved herself free of the building, and army crawled to the nearest cover, then peered back where she had come.

The greenhouse was still. Almost every pane of its west wall had shattered, now. Glass lay everywhere. But whatever tussle Jenkins had just experienced was over. Had he hit his head, collided with his syringe? She got to one knee for a better view. Over the transom of a ruined window, she saw two human shapes. One, most certainly, was Jenkins, passed out from the looks of it. He was sprawled on his side with his eyes shut. His messenger bag lay next to him, partially open, and the rune he'd dug up lay next to his head. A trickle of blood dripped from his temple.

Eileen raised a hand to her mouth. "Are you dead?" she whispered.

"Not quite." Emily again. Her shell-colored hand found Eileen's shoulder. She should have jumped or shuddered, like last time Emily was near. But she didn't. As the hand made contact, what she felt was calm. And that's when Eileen noticed that Emily's hands were bare. She'd left her opera gloves behind. Her uncovered fingers were smooth and elegant with a platinum band on her ring finger. Foreign calligraphy—Gaelic perhaps—decorated its edge.

"He'll recover in an hour," she said. "Take the rune, if you want." She reached to help Eileen up. "You might like to be the one who returns it to my family." Emily smiled. Eileen had never seen the spirit smile.

"Why didn't you come sooner?" Eileen asked. "When I was in the mine shaft or when the Bentley nearly flattened us? There were so many times you could have exposed him." She gestured toward Jenkins.

"It's true, but this way everything's where it's meant to be—that rune stone, the animal steroid, the overdose instructions in those spiral notebooks, the rifle."

She was right. At no other time had these clues assembled so neatly. It was the perfect crime scene. Mad butler tries to maim visiting American. American disorients butler by seeing ghost. Butler faints in fright and hits his head on ancient stone. Loses consciousness. There couldn't be a more ideal place for Emily to take revenge.

"You'll go now, won't you? I mean, you won't visit me again."

She sat on a nearby stone. Her red hair hung loose tonight, and she looked almost alive. Like a teenager out past curfew. "Do you want me to visit you, Eileen?"

"I don't know. I'd miss you, and I don't want to mess anything else up."

"We've repaired what was broken." She touched Eileen's cheek. It was how Ewan touched her, too. Her fingers were snowflakes.

"What about Ewan?" Eileen needed to reunite the two of them, mother and son. How could she reach him, though? She'd looked at her phone a moment before, and the battery had died. Emily touched her fingers to her lips, took a step backward, and blew Eileen a kiss. She was fading into the background again. "He's grown," Emily answered. "He'll have his place, now. And Mother can put me to rest."

She took a final step backward and dissolved in the trees. The chords of her lullaby tinkled a moment, then faded.

"Eileen!"

From the trees where Emily disappeared, Hugh Stalker came bursting through. He wore the yellow rain slicker and carried his own hunting rifle. "Get away from there!"

Relief exploded inside Eileen. "Hugh, thank God. You picked up my call to Ewan's phone? Is he with you? Did he go to the police?"

She wobbled a little. She was sore in almost every joint and scratched and bleeding from the glass. But he wasn't going in to check on Jenkins. Make sure he was good and stunned or whatever. "Hugh, what's the matter?"

He gave the greenhouse a quick glance and nodded at the unconscious butler.

"Um, yeah," Eileen murmured. "I think I'm OK. A few scrapes. But we can take that rune, there. It's pretty valuable, so if you wanted to grab old Jenkins..."

Hugh frowned. "Ewan's missing. I'll make sure Jenkins doesn't go anywhere. Go find Charlie. He comes to you. He and Ewan left this morning. I don't think he's coming back."

Twenty-Seven

The sun broke through the cloud bank as Eileen limped toward the estate's high point, normally with a sightline in four directions. If Charlie and Ewan were on the estate, this was the spot to see them. Her lungs ached from potting shed fumes and the abrasions on her hip felt like a firebrand. She rested against a yew at the top of the hill, where she heard a quiet yelp.

"Charlie!" It wasn't his *hello* yelp, though; he was in distress.

She struggled on over the hilltop toward him.

"Charlie!" she shouted again.

The reply was a low whine. From the direction of the bull's field.

She was almost at the gate to Caedmon's pasture. A final bark came from inside the fence. No sign of Rowena's dog, though. Blood pumped hard behind Eileen's eyes. It would be crazy to climb the fence. But after all that dog had done for her, there wasn't really any choice.

It occurred to her as she put her hand on the first rung of the fence: Was this field the last place Emily drew breath? Well, no, in fact. She'd died at the greenhouse after a massive drug overdose. She probably never knew what killed her, or where her body was dragged.

The clouds were gathering again but from where Eileen stood, nothing moved on the farm or in Caedmon's field. No dog, no bull, no butterfly. *Charlie? Bark, damn it.* A breath of fog touched her face.

Then a yelp from somewhere inside the fence. But where? The light was fading, and she couldn't see the other side of the field. Was Charlie wounded, lying in a clump of weeds? Or hiding, like he did with his scrap of rawhide?

Maybe Caedmon's tied up. He had been at the vet earlier. He could still be restrained. She raised a foot to the first rung of the fence, then one rung more. How would it feel to be stuck with a bull horn? Like a kabob skewer? Swiss Army knife? She thought of the lunatics chasing bulls in Franplona. What did they do that for? It wasn't a sport, but for honor. Are you honorable, Eileen? What you are is insane.

"It'll be all right." Emily's voice. In her head? In the shrubs? Eileen was certain of nothing anymore. Wobbling with the fence rail, she scanned the area for Emily's red hair. There was nothing. Except the voice, again: "I'll keep watch."

"OK," Eileen murmured. "Hope you know what you're doing." She hoisted herself over.

They've got him on downers, Eileen reassured herself. Since the games' fiasco and Temple's accident, Caedmon would be sedated. No chance he'd charge.

Charlie's whine came again, distant this time, from the east, no, no, the north, back up the hill where she'd walked. Fog beaded her eyelashes.

Just look around quickly for Charlie. Check behind the tree and the opposite fence line and get out. She lowered herself onto the ground on the inside of the fence.

"Charlie," she whispered. "Char-leee, come on boy!"

No sound.

Her feet sliced through wet grass, each step was hurdling boulders.

"Charlie!" she said louder. "Come! I've gotta get you home."

A car pulled to a stop some way off. A door opened and closed. No voices, though. No footsteps. Just the sluice of her boots and the metronome behind her ears.

The phone in her coat suddenly buzzed. She shrieked, then muffled her mouth with her hand. But too late. Caedmon was there. Not in his pasture but *outside* the fence where she had been standing two minutes before.

From her side of the fence, Caedmon looked sort of ordinary. He stood on the grass and just looked at her, unbothered. A bored black cow. He wasn't panting or raving. A stalk of grass hung from the side of his mouth. He was alert, but unmoving, unsure what to do with his freedom. *Maybe I could go up with Charlie's leash, and...*

With no warning at all, though, Caedmon charged. Not at Eileen. In the opposite direction, in fact, straight up the hill.

At her dog? Was he there?

"Charlie!" She ran to the fence, climbed back over. "Charlie, come! Where are you? I'm coming. I'll take you home!"

She ran two paces up the hill, stumbled, and fell headfirst into the grass. Inexplicably, in front of her was a pile of tartan. Jenkins's kilt? No, it was a woolen bag, with tubes attached. A bagpipe! Hugh had said Ewan played. If these were his, he was out there—another target for the bull!

"Ewan!" she screamed. "Ewan! The bull's loose!" She picked up the instrument and ran after Caedmon. Faintly she made out his shape. He looked disoriented in the fog and had slowed to a walk in a shallow valley. There, against a dying tree a hundred yards away was Charlie. He crouched low among curling roots.

"Charlie!" Eileen cried.

He turned at her voice but didn't move.

"Eileen." Ewan's voice startled her from the road. "Stay where you are." He approached, but then backed away and turned to Charlie, who cowered beside a leafless tree in a puddle-forged gully. Ewan approached him in a crouch, his hand extended. Charlie went for him like it was the hand of God.

With that joyful dash, Caedmon came to life. He charged at Ewan with a bellow straight from hell, from the depths of an ocean, a BP tanker lost on the North Sea.

"Ewan!" Eileen croaked. She had almost no voice but began to run in their direction. "Get out of there!"

Caedmon closed and Ewan edged sideways to the very edge of the field. In his left arm he hold Charlie. His right hip faced Caedmon, like a matador.

"Run!"

Ten yards between them. Eight.

Suddenly from the fog-bound road a woman sprang. It wasn't Emily. This woman was smaller, less agile, and wore a knot of hair at her neck. With no noise or warning, she ran straight into the path of the bull.

Eileen hid her face in her hands.

But there was no scream upon collision. No thud of impact. What Eileen did hear was a gunshot.

When she finally got the courage to look up, Caedmon was lying on the ground. On the bluff above them stood a solitary figure, whose poncho swung out wide from his body in the wind. A rifle rested in his left hand, the smoking barrel still pointed at the bull. He seemed to nod at Eileen as she watched him, then lowered the weapon across his shoulder and disappeared in the direction of the farm.

Twenty-Eight

"I suppose I should thank you," Lady Rutherford said. Eileen had come to visit after Dr. Marshall gave permission. "You seem to have broken a spell around here. Now that Jenkins and Temple have left us in peace, we'll have a job restructuring the estate and farm. More barley for Dan Stalker, more sheep for Ewan. And Hugh has that wee bullock. There's a chance, with his pedigree, that he may fetch even higher breeding fees than his mad old father."

She took a sip of tea with a shaky hand. Eileen helped her return the teacup to its saucer. Her leap to protect Ewan had pulled several ligaments in her neck. She'd wear a brace for a month. "He had a long life, our Caedmon. Time to give a younger bull the spotlight. Wouldn't you say, Hugh?"

Hugh, standing a few paces from the old lady's chair, agreed. Eileen was surprised to see him in the lady's reception room when she arrived. They had both been summoned, though, *to settle accounts*, according to Clyde, who came for her at the Red House, where she'd been packing for the trip home.

"Hugh." Lady Rutherford smoothed the blanket on her knees and pointed to a glass of water on a side table. He passed her the glass. "Hugh, please explain to Eileen what we were discussing before she arrived. I don't know that she'll believe it if she doesn't hear the story directly from you. Given that my husband withheld Ewan's fortune for so long."

175

Hugh blinked once, then took a step toward the couch in the middle of the room, then considered the rocker. He couldn't seem to decide if he should sit or stand. In the end he remained standing.

"Eileen," he started. But then he reconsidered. "Lady Rutherford, are ye sure you don't want to explain this yourself?"

The lady shook her head.

"All right, then. Lady Rutherford wants me to tell you, Eileen, about what happened to the Stalkers."

"That's right," Lady R. said.

"Not that it's anyone else's affair, mind you." Hugh expelled a long sigh. "Ewan is a Rutherford. No matter what folks have said." He paused again twisting his fingers.

"It's as you say, Hugh. He is a Rutherford," Lady R. reassured him. "And with Jenkins's backdoor dealings unveiled, Ewan finally has the lord's approval for reinstatement as heir. We knew he'd been embezzling, but we hadn't realized he'd also planted fraudulent treasure on our land, nor, of course, that dreadful performance drug he was using."

As far as Eileen knew, Hugh had decided not to tell Lady Rutherford how Jenkins had used it on her daughter and, very likely, on the lord as well. That shock might be one too many for the old lady. The other counts against their butler seemed enough. He had enough charges of fraud and criminal endangerment to warrant a lengthy jail term

"The marriage," Lady R went on, "between Emily and Bruce Stalker was something my husband strictly forbade. He told Emily she'd be disinherited if she pursued it. But then Ewan came along. He changed everything and softened everyone's heart. Except his grandfather's. Unlike the lord, though, I didn't want to turn the Stalkers out of the estate. They'd been farming here for centuries. The compromise was to break up the family."

"So, because he *was* family, Ewan went to school in Edinburgh. Emily wasn't allowed to bring Stalker to the castle, so they moved to the Red House. Bruce and Dan and Hugh went on tending the animals and the farm. For a while, everyone kept their peace."

"Until Jenkins showed up," Hugh said from his place by the window. "He bent the lord. Darkened him. He already hated our da, but

Jenkins made that hatred something worse. Something sorta ghostly. He went and cursed our da one day. After that, the fella got lost in the bottle. I became a parent to Ewan, until me own accident." He rubbed the scar on his temple.

Lady Rutherford crinkled her brow. "It was my idea to send Bruce Stalker to the oil rig until he could sober up. But he never did. He fell off the platform while Ewan was at school. He was never found. A few months after that, Emily died in Caedmon's field. No one realized Jenkins's part, with the doping, until your discovery in the greenhouse—when you, Eileen, found her gloves."

She took another sip of water. "Tell Eileen what really happened with Caedmon, Hugh."

"I am the eldest son. I was s'posed to undo the mess me da made of the farm." Hugh looked Eileen firmly in the eye. "I did not set the bull on anyone. But I can see how someone else could make it look that way. I have the ingredients to sedate the bull for shows and to arouse him, if need be, for breeding. If the drugs are given wrong, the bull can become dangerous, like with the postman and Emily, and supposedly with Andrew Temple, and, almost, with the lady here and me little brother. Of course no one suspected that Jenkins would persuade Temple to fake his *own* accident."

"Or to stampede anyone else who might get in his way," Lady Rutherford added.

Eileen shuddered. She marveled at how many months she, Ewan, the Rutherfords, and Granny had been in such proximity to this lunatic.

"Despite the will Jenkins cobbled together," Lady Rutherford continued, "my grandson is the natural heir. He renounced the title after his parents' death and didn't seem much of a threat to Jenkins at first. And as the son of a commoner, Ewan wasn't suitable, in some opinions, to have a title. Jenkins convinced me to take that opinion, myself, to my eternal shame. What brought things to a head, of course, was the accident."

"Emily's accident?" Eileen asked.

"Another one," the lady explained. "This one involving Hugh, Ewan, and the laird."

"And a rifle!" Eileen interjected. "A gun that fired accidentally."

Hugh frowned in surprise.

"I—I sort of heard about it already." Eileen turned to Hugh. "I know. Sounds crazy but, uh, Emily told me. A boy argues with the lord and accidentally shoots you. Then the lord falls over a cliff."

Lady Rutherford put her hand to her mouth. "She's been circulating, has she?"

"She's very insistent," Eileen murmured.

Hugh rubbed his brow.

"That was the accident where you got your scar?" Eileen asked.

Hugh didn't reply, though, just stared out the castle window.

The Lady sighed. "Come sit by me, Eileen."

She rose and brought her chair closer.

The great lady stroked the satin opera gloves Eileen had returned to her. Moth-eaten though they were, she treated them like an ermine stole. "Lord Rutherford was so badly hurt he never walked again. He changed his will as soon as he could write, through Jenkins, and excised any mention of his grandson. Their relationship truly knocked the sense out of him. Made him totally paranoid. He was afraid of leaving the castle with Jenkins at the helm. He turned his back on all remaining Rutherfords in Scotland. The way Jenkins told it, though, the fall had been planned by Ewan. It was the dark outcome of trusting the lower classes."

"You really believed," Hugh said, with his back still turned, "that a ten-year-old would throw his grandfather off a cliff?"

"An eyewitness saw him," she said.

Hugh laughed. "Right, Jenkins!"

Lady R. lowered her eyes. "For years, though, he was our only friend. The lord had no one visit and went nowhere. Jenkins read to him, helped him in and out of bed, took him to garden shows and Highland Games, succeeded where I'd failed countless times. Made the man feel a lord again. Was it my place to fire such a man?

"Things changed when Caedmon got banned from competition. First just a local one but then more and more. I asked our vet to keep his eye on Jenkins off the record since our bull had never been disqualified from a show before he began on our staff. Turned out both he and Temple had access to Caedmon's feed."

"That's where I came in." Hugh approached them from the window. "Temple started tagging along everywhere with me, offering lifts, company at the pub." He nodded at Eileen. "Supplies went missing from the barn soon after. But I never thought it was actual tampering until recently. An empty syringe found its way in Caedmon's water trough. Temple or Jenkins must have mixed whatever they were cooking into his water, and given how erratic he'd been since even as far back as the lord's accident, I think it's been some six years that those fellas had been doping him."

"So Temple's own accident, you think he staged that?" Eileen said.

"What else?" Lady Rutherford said.

"And then when a stampeding animal didn't scare you back to the States," Hugh went on, "Temple chased you down a mine shaft."

The lady nodded. "Leaving their last act, setting the bull loose on the castle front yard."

"Jenkins must have offered a pretty sweet deal to get Temple so involved." Hugh drummed his fingers on the top of a trolley table. "He'd been a decent chap. Kind to his grandmother, saving wounded squirrels."

"You're right." Eileen stood up from her chair. "Jenkins offered him this." Eileen reached into the pocket of her jacket and brought out the tooled rune stone.

Lady Rutherford's quilt fell off her knees. "That's the Rutherford Rune!" She put her hand to her mouth. "Where did he find that?"

"I saw a copy of it in Temple's house in his curio cabinet. Back a few weeks ago. He said it was a forgery, but I don't actually know if he was sure. He was holding out for authentication, I'll bet, but the risk would be...well, high, if an art dealer thought he was dealing fakes. So he kept that collection kind of quiet."

"So you think this is the real thing?" Lady Rutherford asked. "May I?" She reached for the stone. "And there may be more than one of them?"

Eileen took the artifact to the old lady, who held it like a rare jewel in her fingers.

"I have another stone under my mattress." Eileen bit her lip,

"You're full of surprises!" the lady said.

"Of course, I'll bring that one back to you. They're both from the estate. So they're yours."

Hugh whistled quietly. "Those blokes from London spent months looking for that thing. But Jenkins beat them to it? Or was it you, Eileen?"

"It was Jenkins," the lady answered for her. "In the earth up to his neck, in the garden, among the flower beds. It was just too hard to stop him in the middle of the night. It really is a lovely carving." She turned it over carefully. "I suppose the Romans brought herds with them."

"Temple said it's older," Eileen said. *"Pictish."*

"No wonder the fuss. This one was in Jenkins's belongings?"

"That one, yes," Eileen poured herself more tea. "The carving I found was in the mine—in the service entrance I fell in. It may have been Emily's stone. I heard she played a game hiding it on the estate. The rune you have there, Lady Rutherford, was buried at the abandoned greenhouse. Same place where I found..." She gestured at the threadbare opera gloves in the lady's lap.

There was silence for a moment. Eileen wasn't sure if she should stay. Lady Rutherford had a faraway look about her. A look of remembering, and suffering.

Hugh shifted his weight.

Eileen got up to leave. What remained to be said? Emily was settled, Ewan had regained his title. Though there was no announcement, Eileen's visit was at a close. As she reached for the door to leave, Lady Rutherford made a tiny cough.

"Eileen. Did Emily have a message for me? We didn't part on good terms, and I hope she might think better of me now."

"She said to put the gloves away." Eileen placed a hand on the old lady's shoulder. It was a bold move, and she quickly withdrew.

But the lady grasped for her. There were tears in her eyes. "Come see us again soon, Eileen."

Ewan sat in the doorway of the staff entrance, the door Eileen left the castle through on her last visit. He was chewing a dinner roll. Seeing Eileen approach, he touched his cap to the cook, whose roll he was eating, and stood.

"Ewan!" Eileen tried hard not to grin. "You OK? No fractures, no dislocated arms?"

"I'm fine, lass. And a lot better than some. Mr. Temple's done a runner. But now that Jenkins has squealed, he won't get far. Plus the cops found eight more syringes in his cottage. He wasn't much for destroying evidence. What he *was* good at was faking injuries. He dislocated his shoulder in a pub brawl the night of that *stampede*. Fooled us, eh? Even Dr. Marshall."

They began walking toward the farm. Evening was coming. The air smelled flinty with a mix of coal and cut grass.

"What'll you do now, Ewan?"

The barley had just been mowed. Eileen had watched twenty-five workmen mow, rake, and stack it for the distillery.

"Well, there's a question." Ewan picked up a tree branch and tossed it at the tree line. Charlie, who'd come with him for the walk, tore after the stick. "I might go learn to pipe properly. I never had a lesson, and it deserves a proper go."

"Ewan. I mean with this place? What'll you do with the castle and your title?"

"Och. Right. I suppose they'll expect me to wear the colors more often."

"Your tartan?" she asked. "The girls will love it."

He laughed. "Don't bring that up around Granny. She'll chase them off with a switch."

They walked on in silence for a while.

"Ewan, will I see you again? School starts in a couple weeks. I'm flying home in two days."

He turned a slow circle in the gravel. "You could do better, you know, than a farm lad."

Eileen didn't know how to reply to that. He was hardly a farm lad. "I know you're sort of a prince or whatever now. But could we have a future? You know, if I visit again?"

"I'm tied to the land, lass. I was a farmer before and am even more so as laird. Would it bother you, being bound to the fields?"

Eileen's eyes began to swim. "No, it wouldn't. I'd count the days 'til I could get back." She wiped her eyes roughly. "What will happen to your brothers?"

"Och, they'll carry on. There's calves to raise, a new season of breeding. That'll occupy Hugh. Daphne's sending her niece to help at the farmhouse so Dan can move over full-time to planting and harvesting. He's keen to get his own Scotch label. Us Stalkers, we're men of resource. We'll carry on."

She nodded and reached into her pocket for a Kleenex.

Ewan rubbed the back of her neck. "We'll pick up from here on your next visit. The old lady said you could come any time."

"But I'm a Yank. No title, remember?"

"What? No, you're a Morgan. That's fine stock. A border people, but we'll make do."

"You're a lord, Ewan. Will I really see you again?" They had reached the top of the bluff. The estate sprawled below, the Red House to the west, the castle to the east, and the farm buildings in the valley opposite. The hills rolled in between, jade green in the shadows, lemon yellow in the sun. A thistle down floated overhead, and Eileen caught it between her fingers.

"Blow it out to sea," Ewan said.

She took a breath and blew it over the Red House, past the castle, the coats of arms, the ivy-covered headstones, the tartan, the Gothed-out street kids, out and out again, beyond the wild grey waters, where sixteen lasts forever and Charlie is king again.

Made in the USA
San Bernardino, CA
13 January 2015